The First Two Lives of
Lukas-Kasha

The First Two Lives of Lukas-Kasha

LLOYD ALEXANDER

A YEARLING BOOK

Published by
Dell Publishing Co., Inc.
1 Dag Hammarskjold Plaza
New York, New York 10017

Yearling ® TM 913705, Dell Publishing Co., Inc.

ISBN: 0-440-42784-3

Reprinted by arrangement with E. P. Dutton,
a division of Elsevier-Dutton Publishing Co., Inc.
Printed in the United States of America
First Yearling printing—September 1982

CW

For all who can imagine
that it really happened,
and for all who wish it could

The First Two Lives of
Lukas-Kasha

CHAPTER
🙣 *1* 🙣

Curled in a heap of wood shavings, Lukas was comfortable except for the carpenter's boot in his ribs and the carpenter's voice in his ear.

"Wake up! I've got something to tell you."

Lukas crawled out of the shavings, rubbing sleep and sawdust from his eyes. He unrolled the cap he had wadded up for a pillow. Nicholas stumped to his workbench and beckoned the lad to follow.

"I've been thinking," Nicholas began.

"What?" cried Lukas. "You could ruin your brain!"

The carpenter ignored this, cleared his throat, and began again.

"I've been thinking that I'm getting no younger. Suppose, now, I told you I want an apprentice. A quick, strong boy I can teach my trade. When I'm gone, he'd be town carpenter in my place, and make what he will of himself."

"You've already made the boy a carpenter." Lukas yawned. "Why wake me up to tell me that?"

"Blockhead! Must I hammer every nail? It's you I'm talking about."

Lukas burst out laughing. "Me? Sneezing sawdust? Pounding my thumbs flat?"

"You idler, I do you a favor and you take it like the plague. Honest work—"

"Stop, stop! I can't bear it!" Lukas glanced around, then whispered, "I've never told anyone—who wants news like that to spread?—but I have a terrible ailment. Work makes me ill. Even the word gives me fits." He rolled his eyes and clutched his belly. "Aie! One's coming on me now. Hurry, Nicholas! The antidote! A broiled sausage! Two, for safety!"

"Quit playing the fool. Is that how you carry on when you're offered a decent living?"

"I suppose so." Lukas grinned. "It never happened before. What about the sausage?"

"None," said Nicholas. "No more. You'll see, it will be for your own good."

"That means it's boring, it hurts, or it tastes bad."

The carpenter dug into his purse. "From now on, you work for what you get." He took out a silver penny and handed it to Lukas. "I'll give you that each week for wages. No apprentice gets more; most of them, less."

"Handsome," Lukas admitted. "You're a prince of good fellows, even without the sausage. But, my ailment—"

"Take it in advance," the carpenter said. "Think on it."

"As soon as I have a moment to spare." Pocketing the coin, Lukas tipped his cap over one eye and was into the street before his would-be master could say a word more.

Since it was market day, he hurried to the town square. Old Nicholas had called him an idler. Lukas, nevertheless, had many virtues. Generous, he shared every morsel of gossip he collected. Diligent, in a single night he chalked the Mayor's portrait on a dozen walls. Frugal, he took only one holiday and made it last all year. He loved to laugh, to sing, to dance on his hands, which he did frequently. He loved to eat, which he did seldom. He loved to sleep, which he did wherever it suited his fancy; though he best liked the carpenter shop. Nicholas, for all his grumbling, usually set out a plate of leftovers.

He also made it his duty to know everything that was happening in Zara-Petra. Over the shouts of vegetable sellers and fishmongers, an unfamiliar jingling and rattling caught his ears, and he slipped through the crowd to the middle of the square.

There, a gaily painted, canvas-topped wagon drawn by a donkey had halted near the town pump. Astride the donkey sat a skinny-armed ape dressed in crimson pantaloons and a vest studded with glass beads. The creature rattled a tambourine, tossed and caught it again. Then he sprang to his feet, danced a few nimble steps,

[3]

and jumped head over heels to land on the donkey's back.

These antics made Lukas laugh so heartily and so absorbed him that several moments passed before he realized the canvas flap had been hoisted up. Out stepped a sparrowlike little man with a stringy beard and a narrow, beaky face. He unlatched the tailboard, transforming it into a pair of wooden steps. Then, throwing back his threadbare cloak, he clapped for attention and in a scratchy voice announced himself: Battisto the Magnificent.

"What's it going to be?" wondered Lukas. "Hair oil or a cure for bunions?"

The ape, meantime, loped along the edge of the crowd, holding out his empty tambourine. The townsfolk were too shrewd to pay for undemonstrated marvels, and Battisto's bearing inspired no outburst of generosity. A few onlookers began drifting away.

"If this fellow gets anyone to open a purse," Lukas told himself, "that's his best miracle for the day."

Nevertheless, he did not want to miss any chance for amusement. So, as the ape drew closer, Lukas nudged the baker's apprentice, who was munching a wedge of pie.

"Go ahead, give the poor beast something. He looks like he could stand a meal better than you."

"You do it," challenged the apprentice. "Put up your own money. As if you could."

The ape rattled his tambourine. Battisto, it seemed, was not going to perform without cash in hand. Lukas shrugged, pulled the silver penny from his pocket and tossed it into the tambourine. The eyes of the baker's boy popped, exactly as Lukas intended.

The ape jabbered gleefully, bowed to the ground, then somersaulted into the wagon, where he offered the coin to his master. Battisto squinted at the silver piece, bit it, and flung it into the air along with the tambourine. Both vanished. The onlookers murmured mild approval.

Battisto snapped his fingers and the ape scuttled behind the canvas to drag out a large, battered cook pot. The conjurer turned the vessel upside down to prove it was empty, then set it on the wagon bed. As if unsure what he might find, he thrust in a hand and fumbled out a string of kerchiefs; next, a bunch of paper flowers; and, lastly, a scruffy chicken that cackled indignantly as it flapped to roost on the donkey's head.

There was a pattering of applause. "The chicken's not a bad touch," Lukas said to himself. "The rest, any rascal in the world can do."

At the same time, one of the town militiamen waved his musket and called out, "Come on, whiskers! Show us something new."

Battisto raised his arms. "Dear friends, forgive me. I should have known you were not mere country bumpkins. There's no putting you off with childish diversions. You demand nothing less than my wonder of wonders, a marvel to change your very life."

"Now," thought Lukas, "is when he trots out the hair oil."

The ape had already taken a pail from the wagon and filled it at the pump. He presented it to Battisto, who, without ceremony, poured the water into the pot.

"I shall require the assistance of one of you," he declared. "Who is willing? I warn you, he must be bold enough to face every peril, to dare the unknown. Strong, quick-witted—"

"That's our Kasha!" guffawed one of the idlers.

"He's fearless!" shouted another. "I've seen him attack a roast mutton with his bare hands."

Laughing and hooting, the onlookers pressed Lukas closer to the wagon. He needed no urging, since he enjoyed giving a performance as much as watching one. He bowed with mock reverence, flexed his arms in a comical show of brawn, then stood on his hands and kicked his heels in the air. The crowd whistled and the baker's boy called out:

"That's right, Kasha! Show us where your wits are. In your feet!"

This brought more laughter and catcalls. Lukas righted himself, but before he could fling a proper insult at the baker's dunce, Battisto motioned for him to climb the steps.

Having spent his only coin for entertainment, entertainment there would be, even if Lukas had to provide it himself. "No offense," he said under his breath to Battisto, "but if you want to peddle whatever you're peddling, you'll have to liven up your show. Tell me the trick. I'll make you look like a real wonder-worker."

[6]

Battisto only studied him carefully. "Do you come willingly? Do you put yourself altogether in my hands?"

Facing the mountebank, Lukas found him taller than he had seemed. The little man's eyes glittered as he cocked his head to one side. Instead of a sparrow, he resembled a hawk. Lukas shifted uneasily. But, with half the town looking on, there was no way to back out.

He nodded. "What's your game, then? You'll saw me in half? Send me up in a puff of smoke?"

"Look into the water," Battisto said. "Closer," he urged, as Lukas crouched and peered in. "Closer yet."

Lukas felt the conjurer's bony hand on the nape of his neck. Before he could brace himself or turn away, his head was plunged into the vessel.

Brine filled his nose and mouth. He struggled to clear his bursting lungs, and jumped to his feet only to feel his legs give way beneath him. He blinked open eyes that smarted with salt water.

Battisto had vanished. All the town had vanished.

Lukas, alone under a blinding sun, was drowning in the sea.

CHAPTER

❈ *2* ❈

*T*oo busy saving his skin to wonder how Battisto had done him such a turn, Lukas flailed his arms and kicked his heels. As the undertow grappled him, he fought to keep his head above water. Close by, he glimpsed a line of cliffs and struck out for them. Able to swim nearly as fast as he could bolt down an alley, Lukas held his own against the waves.

Their buffeting, however, grew stronger. Near the shore, foam spewed from the gaps in a jetty of rocks. A whirlpool sucked him in and so battered him he felt Battisto had plucked him from the sea only to plunge him into some giant's churn. He clutched at the rocks, but the tide ripped his hands away, seized him, toyed with him, wrapped him in trails of seaweed; and at last, beyond any effort of his own, flung him headlong onto the beach.

Gasping and choking, Lukas crawled out of the surf and, arm-weary, sprawled full-length until his breath came back. He sat up, peeled the weeds from his face, and laughed until his sides ached.

"Marvelous! Perfect! Battisto, I take off my cap to you."

So he would have done, but his cap, along with most of his clothing, was gone. The waves had stripped him close to naked. What was left of his breeches hung in tatters. His shirt, threadbare to begin with, was no more than a rag on his shoulders.

He shook his head in admiration. Once, at the town fair, he had seen a traveling hypnotist with a glance so powerful he could make his unwitting victims dance jigs or crow like roosters. Battisto must be a master of such trickery. The illusion here was amazing. The sand felt gritty under his feet. The dazzling sun, the ocean seemed real beyond a doubt. He had even begun trembling, and it was all he could do to keep his teeth from chattering.

"Enough! Wake me up now. You'll have me imagine I'm coming down with the chills."

He shut his eyes a moment and waited. When he opened them again, he was still shuddering on the beach. His ribs hurt not from laughter but from welts and bruises.

"Hurry up, you rascal. This dream you've put me into—it smarts!"

Nothing changed. The tumble of rocks, the cliff, the foaming eddies all stayed as they had been.

"Don't wake me, then," said Lukas. "I'll wake myself."

He gave himself a pinch on the arm, then another. This failing, he boxed his own ears and tugged his hair until his eyes watered.

Panic rising, he buffeted himself as mercilessly as the waves. The blows fell solid and real. This was no dream. He was here, exactly where he saw himself to be. Nor was there any certainty the peddler would or could bring him back.

He ran to the water's edge and cried Battisto's name at the sky. The wind swept his voice away. He shook his fist, roared, and shouted himself hoarse. His answer was only the mewing of gulls. He fell to his knees and flung up handfuls of sand as if he could dig his way home. By turn, he cursed and begged, commanded and pleaded, all in vain. Lukas buried his face in his hands.

The sound of hoofbeats made him lift his head. Further down the beach, a white horse was galloping toward him. He stood, waved his arms, and ran to halt the steed.

Mane flying, eyes rolling, the horse reared and struck at him with its forelegs. Lukas tumbled clear and called out to the rider.

It was a girl, wearing rough cotton trousers and tunic. He put out a hand to catch the bridle, then saw she rode without saddle or harness.

"Tell me," cried Lukas. "Where am I?"

The girl stared for an instant. In her sunburnt face, her yellow eyes glared at him. She spun her mount aside. Without a word, she clapped bare heels against the horse's flanks.

"Wait! Hold on a minute!" Lukas called, as horse and rider plunged away.

"To the devil with you, then," he shouted after the girl, who soon galloped out of sight. "Little wretch. There's a friendly welcome to—to wherever this is."

His vexation at least had shaken him out of his despair, and he turned his mind to the practical question of what to do.

"If I keep walking inland," he thought, "I'm bound to find people sooner or later." A town, he told himself, was a town. And there, Lukas felt, he could manage very well indeed.

He had no time to put his plan to work. A troop of horsemen in pointed helmets were bearing down on him at full tilt. Some broke away to follow the girl. The rest were brandishing long, curved blades at him. In these circumstances, he did the only sensible thing. He took to his heels.

He scrambled up the rocks. Gravel tore at his bare feet, but he pressed higher, deliberately choosing the sheerest face of the cliff where the horses could not follow.

When he looked back, the riders were no longer in sight. But his relief was short-lived. The troop had found an easier way up the other side of the cliff. He could make out the leader's white turban flashing through piles of boulders.

His flight had brought him to the crest. Below lay the sea, churning around the rocks of the jetty. He could go neither forward nor back. The narrowing trail had forced the riders to dismount and climb after him on foot.

He cast around for some defense. His only hope was somehow to block the path before his pursuers clambered through. His eye fell on the boulders half-buried in the earth. He gripped one and bent all his strength trying to dislodge and send it rolling into the gap. He tugged and wrestled and flung his weight against the rock. It began to shift in its bed. But the same instant he felt it loosen, his fingers slipped and he went sprawling backward. His head struck a ledge as solidly as the town smith had ever struck hammer on anvil.

Lukas sighed happily, savoring the delicious moment between waking and opening his eyes. He burrowed deeper into the pillows, pulled the coverlet around his shoulders. Then he sat bolt upright. His head throbbed. He fingered the lump on the back of his skull. Battisto, the sea, the girl's angry eyes, the horsemen—as best he could make out, he was now on a couch of carpets piled with cushions. He had been clothed in a loose shirt, embroidered vest, and trousers. In front of him hung a curtain. He jumped to his feet and cautiously drew it aside.

Brightness dazzled him. Shafts of sunlight fell from

rows of high arched windows between gleaming pillars. He saw, crowding the long chamber, men in brocaded coats whose skirts swept the tiled floor, and bejeweled women in trailing silks of red, green, and pink. On the other side of the alcove stood ranks of guards costumed like those who had been chasing him.

"And from the look of things," Lukas told himself, "they finally caught me."

Suddenly, horns blared, cymbals clashed, and such a din battered his ears that he was sure his head would split from the confusion both inside and outside it. The watching throng dropped to their knees and, to his further bewilderment, began kissing the ground between their hands.

A slender, black-bearded man had been standing a few paces in front of Lukas. His magnificent costume and elegant bearing indicated high rank.

"I'm in trouble already," groaned Lukas. However, the illustrious figure also dropped to his knees and bowed his turbaned head.

"Wonder of the Age!" he cried. "May your steps be ever fortunate. May your shadow never be less! O Master of the World! O Fountainhead of Virtue!"

"One thing sure," thought Lukas, "whoever he is, he's never been to Zara-Petra."

The official rose to his feet and came closer.

"How shall you be called, O Repository of All Merit?" he asked. "Under what name shall you command your servants?"

"Name?" stammered Lukas. "Why—what everyone calls me: Kasha."

The courtier turned and stretched out his arms.

"Behold!" he cried. "Behold Kasha, King of Abadan!"

CHAPTER

❦❦ 3 ❦❦

*A*re they lunatics or what?" thought Lukas. "I no sooner hear the name of this place than they tell me I'm king of it. Anyhow, it's a better welcome than I had on the beach."

Having so far kept his head on his shoulders wonderfully relieved his mind. Nevertheless, he felt uneasy. For one thing, not in his wildest dreams had he imagined being king of anything. For another, if these courtiers were serious—which made him wonder about their sanity— there might be another King of Abadan, the real one, arriving at any moment. "And when he sees me warming his throne—"

The courtier addressed him again:

"O King, live forever. I am Shugdad Mirza, Chief Minister, Grand Vizier to the Center of the Universe, if this please Your Majesty."

The wish that he should live forever pleased Lukas

greatly. Shugdad was another matter. The man was elegant in his robe of gold cloth and gem-studded belt; and handsome in a sour sort of way. His beard covered much of his face, and Lukas could not be certain of the expression on Shugdad's mouth, but he doubted that it was smiling.

The Vizier, in addition, looked solemn and hardworking, which troubled Lukas immediately. The smooth voice made Lukas feel as if he were having his nose wiped with a silk handkerchief. However, the more Shugdad kept on with his declarations of obedience and devotion, the more Lukas was persuaded he had something disagreeable in mind.

"He's not happy to see me," thought Lukas. "I don't know why. He doesn't even know me."

Meanwhile, the audience chamber had been cleared of all but a group of courtiers waiting near the alcove. The Vizier now presented the first of them, a heavy-shouldered, spike-bearded man with a brutal face.

"This is Nahdir Aga, your Commander of Guards," declared the Vizier. "He desires to beg your forgiveness."

"Oh?" said Lukas. "What for?"

"It was Commander Nahdir who led his guards in your pursuit," answered Shugdad. "A deplorable error."

Though kneeling humbly, Nahdir half-grinned, baring the edges of his teeth. To Lukas, he appeared not at all penitent, in spite of his words.

"The orders were misunderstood. The fault is mine, O King. Do with me as you will."

"I'll think of something," answered Lukas.

Resolving to keep an eye on this fellow, Lukas turned his attention to the remaining functionaries. There was a Royal Chamberlain, a Keeper of the Seals, a Master of Protocol, and a dozen others. But after the first three or four, Lukas gave up trying to keep them straight in his head. The names of these high officers were as baffling as their occupations, and his tongue went into knots over them.

"Try saying names like those three times in a hurry," Lukas told himself, "and I could break out in a rash."

The last official was the Court Astrologer, Locman, peering and blinking, looking vaguely bewildered as if he had miscounted his fingers. Locman was bony, spindle-shanked, and a little humped with age. His grizzled hair straggled from beneath a tall cap of lamb's fleece. A string of wooden beads girdled the white robe sagging at his heels like a crone's nightgown. Having hobbled forward and paid his homage, the Astrologer beamed at him.

"Center of the Universe, I am delighted to say that your coming has been exactly as I foretold."

"When I got up this morning, being Center of the Universe was the last thing I had in mind," replied Lukas. "Are you telling me you knew this would happen?"

"All my calculations proved it beyond a doubt," answered Locman. "Is it not written: The magpie scolds the raven, but the nightingale sings to the rose?"

"How's that again? No, never mind. Tell me, did your reckonings show I might have had my head cut off?"

"As for that regrettable incident, no, Master of the World, that was not specifically included in my prognostications. Nahdir Aga meant you no harm. That is to say, he would have meant you no harm had he known who you truly were. He pursues his duties with vigor. He mistook you for a runaway. How fortunate I arrived when I did, and was able to prevent embarrassment to all concerned.

"I say fortunate, Wonder of the Age. But is it not, instead, a simple matter of destiny accomplished as it must be? Without wishing to distress you personally, I may suggest that even if Nahdir had accomplished his mistaken purpose, it would still have been in perfect accord—"

"Wait a minute," Lukas broke in. "You're saying that if you hadn't come along when you did, whatever happened would have been what was supposed to happen?"

"Precisely, O King," replied Locman, delighted. "You have grasped the very heart of my science. Indeed, it is written—"

"We'll talk about that later." Lukas motioned the Court Astrologer to rise. He was anxious to settle a more immediate concern. On top of being half-drowned, nearly killed, knocked senseless, and hailed as Center of the Universe, he had missed breakfast.

"Let's see if I'm really king here," he told himself. He summoned Shugdad and ordered the Grand Vizier to bring him food.

"To hear is to obey," declared Shugdad, with some distaste. "Only tell me, O Center of the Universe, what may tempt your appetite."

"Easy," said Lukas. "Bring whatever there is."

The Vizier clapped his hands, and a procession of cooks, saucemakers, and confectioners soon marched through the hall. One after another, they presented Lukas with gold basins and bowls for his approval. The vessels overflowed with bits of spiced fowl and pungent rice; morsels of meat roasted on skewers; and almonds, raisins, and sweets in such a stream that Lukas, though ravenous, could scarcely keep up with it.

Pausing to regain his strength for a new assault on this endless feast, he called Locman to him again. His hunger was more than satisfied, but not his curiosity, and he felt easier with the Court Astrologer than with the Grand Vizier.

"Locman," he said, trying to choose his words carefully so as not to appear altogether an idiot, "what I have to know is this: Where am I?"

Locman blinked his watery eyes. "Why, Center of the Universe, you are where you belong, in your kingdom."

"Yes, I understand that," said Lukas. "I mean, here, now, this very moment."

The Court Astrologer seemed more puzzled than before. "O King, you are in your palace. Where else should you be?"

"The place, the town," Lukas persisted, though fearing this line of questioning would further baffle the Astrologer.

"The Royal City of Shirazan," replied Locman. "The matchless pearl of all the realm—"

"That's what I mean," said Lukas. "It's called Shirazan? And this country is Abadan? I'm truly supposed to rule it?"

"Naturally," said Locman. "But never trouble your mind, Wonder of the Age. You have many to share your burden. Myself, for one, and all your ministers of state. Your people are loyal and obedient—"

"That's good news, anyway," said Lukas.

"Oh, yes, River of Compassion," Locman went on, "your people will love and admire you. Indeed, they are required to. You have governors, vice-governors, magistrates, vice-magistrates, judges, constables, and executioners all to make sure they do."

Locman hesitated, then reluctantly admitted, "It is true, the Province of Bishangar—ah, these northern tribes and their self-styled King have been ever contrary and troublesome. As they say in the bazaar, cross a Bishangari, deal with a devil. Some scholars believe the thinness of the mountain air has disturbed their brains; others, that they have allowed too much authority to their women and thereby set everything askew. In any case, they are ferocious madmen in their hills."

Hardly reassured, Lukas pressed on. "Now, then, you said my coming was foretold. How could that be? Was there no King of Abadan already on the throne?"

"Twenty days ago, the old King died without an heir," Locman replied, "and without kinsmen of royal blood. In such an event, by law and custom, a sacred duty falls on the Court Astrologer to determine the next King. Where he shall be found and how recognized. I consulted, therefore, my books and charts, observed the skies, employed all the elements of my science, and arrived at the unmistakable conclusion that the new King of Abadan would be discovered sitting under a fig tree.

"Indeed, such a one was found. However, he had been eating the figs and had choked on one of them. Redrawing my charts, I then understood that the true King waited on a peak in the eastern mountains. This, too, came to pass; though, deplorably, he had fallen meanwhile, into a ravine and fatally damaged himself. I studied and reckoned again, and saw beyond any doubt that on this very day the new King of Abadan would arise from the sea. And so you have done."

Locman, delighted as a child by his prophecy at last fulfilled, showed no inclination to ask where Lukas had come from and what, to begin with, he was doing in the sea. Lukas, content to leave matters where they stood, continued his questioning:

[21]

"And, Locman, that—embarrassment with Nahdir. Why should he have taken me for a runaway?"

"He saw you with a Bishangari slave girl who had stolen a horse and escaped the palace only a little time before. I had been following Nahdir to the shore, to attend your coming. Nahdir saw you first. His mind works hastily. But, O King, to give him his due, you were not, shall we say, regally garbed. Thus, before I could stop him, he assumed you were in some way leagued with her as an accomplice: perhaps a sweetheart or a slave yourself."

"Was she caught?"

"Alas," replied Locman, "not yet. And the horse was quite valuable."

Shugdad now approached, and with much ceremony begged the Center of the Universe to favor other chambers of the palace with his presence. Lukas had stuffed himself to bursting and gladly would have taken a nap for dessert, but Locman's account had convinced him these people were in earnest; that he was, in their eyes, King of Abadan; and he was eager to inspect his domain.

He set off, then, with Locman on one side, Shugdad on the other, and the ministers of state bringing up the rear. The Shirazan Palace seemed bigger than all Zara-Petra, and its splendors were dazzling: endless halls of gleaming tile, domes of alabaster, vaulted chambers, inner courtyards, a maze of gardens. The Royal Baths alone could have taken in the whole town square.

Finally, with the best will in the world, Lukas could

absorb no more. His legs faltered, his eyelids drooped, he yawned unregally, and announced he could go no further, though Locman assured him he had seen less than half his residence.

He was conducted to private apartments which held as many chambers and vestibules as the Town Hall. Musicians played lutes and sweet wind instruments in an anteroom where perfumes wafted from smouldering braziers. Attendants waited to lead him to his sleeping quarters. Lukas dismissed his ministers and unceremoniously flung himself onto his Royal Couch.

Alone, exhausted though he was, he could not keep from laughing gleefully. He was sure he had at last seen to the bottom of the day's bewilderments.

"Battisto, you rascal, now I catch on to what you were up to all along. You wanted to do me a favor. Something marvelous, just as you said. And you did warn me there'd be danger. But what a holiday! My thanks to you. I've already had more than my penny's worth. If Nicholas could see me now!

"Or," he added, "if I could see him." Lukas, who had no home, choked a little with homesickness. Nevertheless, he swallowed the lump, telling himself to enjoy things while he could. With that, he rolled over and fell gloriously asleep.

∞ *4* ∞

Next day, Lukas was still convinced Battisto had arranged all this for his personal delight. He began his pleasures by commanding to be shown his Royal City. Locman had called Shirazan a matchless pearl. Lukas would no doubt have admired it had he been able to see it.

Instead, after being robed in regal finery, his head swathed in a jeweled turban, a gem-studded dagger in a sash about his waist, he was conducted to an inner courtyard and handed into a carrying chair. Half a dozen bearers hoisted it up and set off through the palace gate. Shugdad, astride a black horse, rode ahead; Nahdir and his cavalry galloped alongside. Locman, miscalculating the hour of departure, had to be left behind.

The gold lattice enclosing the Royal Vehicle scarcely allowed a glimpse of its passenger. Borne through crowds cheering and prostrating themselves before a near-invisible occupant, Lukas told himself Battisto's ape might as well be in his place with no one the wiser. He could only poke his fingers through the grille and acknowledge his subjects with all the majesty this gesture allowed. Of the city itself, he had a blurred impression of spires, domes, towers of rainbow colors, massive stone walls flanked by pillars, a lofty archway, a heavy gate. Despite the sun, the pinnacles seemed cold and sharp as icicles.

The only quarter he found agreeably disordered, noisy, and reeking with tantalizing smells was Shirazan Bazaar. It was so jammed with hagglers and hawkers, beggars, donkeys, and bawling pack camels that Nahdir's officers had to beat a passage with the flats of their swords. Lukas pricked up his ears, his eyes brightened, and he knocked on the sides of his litter, calling for his bearers to halt and let him out. The command went unheard or unheeded. Moments later, frustrated, he was jogged back to the palace.

There, attendants whisked him away to the Royal Baths to be scrubbed, rubbed, soaked by turn in pools of icy and scalding water; thumped, scraped, kneaded, oiled, perfumed, and recostumed in fresh clothing. He had never been so alarmingly clean. But he still itched for a closer look at the bazaar.

The Grand Vizier, however, explained that custom forbade a King of Abadan to set foot on ground beyond the palace confines, except in time of war.

"In that case," said Lukas, "I decree a new law. The King of Abadan goes when, where, and how he pleases."

"Center of the Universe," replied Shugdad, "laws are easily changed, but not customs. At some other occasion, it would be fitting if you pleased to go escorted on horseback. The Commander of Guards will serve you in this."

"Between Nahdir's jolly company or being caged up like a traveling cat, there's not much choice," Lukas muttered.

Until he could think of some scheme to avoid the ridiculous restriction, he made up for it in other ways. Once he got used to the shock of cleanliness, he plunged into the Royal Baths and swam and splashed to his heart's content. The Royal Tailors continually fitted him with new and ever more splendid raiment. Lukas, who never had more than one pair of breeches to his name and whose few undergarments were in a constant state of disaster, now changed clothes whenever the mood struck him. Never having eaten his fill, he stuffed himself with sweetmeats, cakes, and perfumed sherbets from the Royal Cooks.

"Being King is a dangerous trade," he told himself. "If this keeps on, I could lose my appetite."

When he wearied of bathing, feasting, and trying on new robes of state, he walked in the Royal Gardens. After a time, the fragrance of rose and jasmine grew stifling. "These gardens could stand a few weeds," he said, "just to liven things up. Those peacocks are handsome, but I'd like a parrot better. Then at least I'd have a sensible conversation."

Shugdad was a tireless, skillful courtier, but the less he saw of him the more comfortable Lukas felt. The Vizier's presence always brought a chill. Nahdir was worse. The Commander of Guards, Lukas decided, had been born brutal. More than once Lukas saw him seize a riding whip and thrash one of his own captains.

Locman was good-natured company, but he seldom talked of anything but his astrological calculations.

"All portents are excellent, Center of the Universe," Locman declared one morning, spreading out his charts of Lukas's daily horoscope. "Everything in its place, as it should be. Observe this perfection of symmetry and balance. Here, the stars make their grand circuit. And here, this constellation appears precisely as it is supposed to. Thus, all is known and predicted with marvelous exactitude. Allow me to draw your attention to this fascinating comet."

The Astrologer pored happily over his diagrams. Lukas had been thinking of something else.

"The runaway girl, that day on the beach—"

"Is that what we were speaking of?" The Astrologer blinked. "Forgive me, I must have lost the thread of your illustrious remarks. I was under the impression the subject was comets."

"It just came to mind," said Lukas. Though, in fact, his recollection of the girl had been like a splinter in his finger, irksome but impossible to ignore. "I only wondered if she was ever caught."

Locman tugged his beard as though to wrench himself away from his comet and set his thoughts on earthly matters. "Ah—yes, O King, I recall that she was."

"I'd like to see her," Lukas said offhandedly. "Can you have her sent here?"

"Naturally, as the King commands it. The Mistress of Slave Women will be instructed to bring this individual into your presence."

Lukas remembered the slave mistress as a remarkably overweight lady of the court, who was continually popping candied rose petals into her mouth. "There's a little too much of that one for a single audience," said Lukas. "I'll see the girl alone."

"This will be done," said Locman, with some hesitation. "It is, you should know, not altogether according to etiquette to give a Bishangari slave a private audience. On the other hand, it would be quite correct for you to make the girl your personal property."

"I don't want to own her," said Lukas, "I just want to talk to her."

Assuring him it would be arranged, the Astrologer withdrew. As the day passed, Lukas grew certain that Locman, absorbed in his planetary speculations, had forgotten. Next afternoon, however, the Royal Chamberlain ushered in the girl, and announced with obvious disdain, "As the King commanded, here is the one who calls herself Nur-Jehan."

Instead of flinging herself to the ground like his other subjects, Nur-Jehan remained standing, head high, studying Lukas as if he were a bug on a pin rather than a king on a throne. The sleeveless robe that she wore tied at the waist with a scarf made her appear angular, even rawboned. Her tawny hair hung loose around a broad forehead, sunburnt and freckled. She would have been plain except for the startling eyes, yellow as a cat's, that she fixed upon him; a gaze, Lukas realized, that was making him intensely uncomfortable.

Since she did not speak, he grasped at some way to begin, and asked how long she had been a slave.

The girl stiffened. "I am not a slave."

"I beg your pardon," said Lukas. "They told me you were."

"Does that make me one? Do they not call you 'Center of the Universe'?"

The girl was watching him steadily. Lukas wondered how she had managed to insult him so neatly.

He thought it safer to change the subject and began again. "A while ago, on the beach. You may not remember—"

"I remember exactly." Nur-Jehan's tone led him to believe that among her memories this was not the fondest.

"Yes, well, we both were having our troubles. That was a fine horse you stole."

"Rakush was not stolen. We are not horse thieves like the Abadanis. Rakush is mine. He shall make his way to Bishangar. I sent him there when I knew I would be captured again. Otherwise, he would have fought to the death for me, as he tried to do when we were taken in the hill country."

Lukas grinned at her. "You're a brigand, then? I'm told all Bishangaris are brigands."

"So we are. In the eyes of Abadan."

"No, seriously," said Lukas, "you're a village girl? What did you do before you were captured? You ride well, anyhow."

"As do all of us. Does the King wish to inform himself in the ways of Bishangar? I doubt that. The slave mistress is not pleased that I have been called here without her. This will cost me a beating. A bad bargain if the King has nothing worth saying to me."

"I'll see to it you won't be mistreated. I thought I might be able to help you."

"The King desires to be helpful? Then stop killing us."

"I don't know much about Abadan and Bishangar," Lukas admitted. "I haven't been King long enough. I mean, I want to help you here, in the palace."

"Then return me to the slave quarters."

For all his good intentions, Lukas felt he was coming out badly. This girl, he decided, was rude, evil tempered, and ungrateful. On top of that, she kept the upper hand with no effort at all.

"You know," he said, "as things seem to be arranged here, all I need to do is drop a hint that the King would be pleased to have a certain Bishangari as a private possession."

"Yes, that is the King's privilege," said Nur-Jehan, "but I assure the King he will wish he had not exercised it."

She said nothing more. Lukas finally called the Chamberlain and told him the audience was over. The only thing that pleased him was that he had seen the last of her.

But he still smarted from their meeting. There must be, he was sure, some way to make the impudent wretch take better notice of him. "Are they all like that in her country?" he wondered. "If they are, I don't think I'd enjoy visiting."

When Shugdad arrived with papers requiring the Royal Hand and Seal, Lukas demanded to know more about the Bishangaris.

The Grand Vizier told him much the same as Locman, adding that they were stiff-necked, arrogant, and past any hope of being tamed.

"Yes," muttered Lukas, "I found that out."

"Their King," continued the Vizier, "as he calls himself, is one named Ardashir. He is no more than a chieftain of brigands, a thorn in the side of Abadan. But a thorn that will be plucked out. How fitting, Wonder of the Age, that you raise the question. Speed the day when you destroy them to the last man, woman, and child."

"Hold on a minute. Who says 'destroy'?"

He shuddered at how easily Shugdad could speak of wiping out a whole province. "No, that's lunacy. Let this Ardashir, whoever he is, go about his business, brigand or whatever. My sense of it is that we're the ones attacking his people, not the other way round."

"They must be broken once and for all," the Vizier insisted. "Then, at last, Your Majesty will possess the Mountains of Ramayan."

"Now it's mountains!" returned Lukas. "Possess them? What do you mean to do, shovel them up and haul them to Abadan?"

The Grand Vizier smiled patiently. "Perhaps the King is unaware. The Bishangaris are too ignorant to profit from the wealth under their feet. Their mountains are rich in gold, silver, and jewels. It would be poor stewardship to leave such treasure in the keeping of wild asses and mountain goats."

"So it's not that Ardashir's a brigand, but a rich brigand," replied Lukas. "I should have known. Your eyes get beady whenever you talk about money, did you realize that? No, I'm sorry to disappoint you, but I want no part of a bloodletting. A little skulduggery once in a while, if nobody gets hurt, that's one thing. Killing is out of the question."

"Permit your servant to remind you that the good of your kingdom is your solemn duty. You need not concern yourself. I and your Council of War will do all that is required. You will not be obliged to take command in the field unless you so choose; which I do not advise."

"Oh, I'll take command!" exclaimed Lukas. "Right now. And order you, Grand Vizier, to have this nonsense ended."

"The King," replied Shugdad, "will do no less than his duty."

"So will the Grand Vizier. You'll do exactly as I say."

Shugdad seemed about to reply, but instead bowed to the ground, murmured a formal courtesy, and withdrew. Lukas had the strong impression his order would be conveniently forgotten.

"That fellow may talk like a silk handkerchief," muttered Lukas, "but I wouldn't be surprised if he kept a razor under it."

Much as he hated to admit it, he felt suddenly frightened. He sat for a time, puzzling what to do. Then he clapped a hand to his head:

"Idiot! I keep forgetting I'm the King! Of course! Nothing easier."

With that, he sent for Locman. It took some while for the Astrologer to appear. Lukas had planned to enjoy the rest of the afternoon in the Royal Baths, never reckoning on matters of state spoiling matters of pleasure. And so, when the Astrologer finally hobbled in, Lukas began without ado. Pacing back and forth, he frankly told the sage that he distrusted Shugdad, that there would be ill will between them, and declared, "I want him sacked. How do I do it?"

Locman thought for a moment or two. "Very easily. There should be, in the Royal Granary, many sacks large enough to fit him. If not, the Royal Tailors—"

"Not put *in* one!" cried Lukas. "Sacked! Thrown out! Sent away!"

"That is a different matter." Locman frowned. "Wonder of the Age, it cannot be done."

"What do you mean?" burst out Lukas. "In my land, a baker's apprentice can be tossed out on his ear for burning a loaf. Or a scullery maid for breaking crockery."

"That is true here, also," replied Locman, "but only of the lower orders. A Grand Vizier cannot be dismissed."

"You mean I'll have him on my back forever?"

"Not at all," said Locman. "He cannot be dismissed. That would be an unspeakable, unthinkable disgrace. However, quite honorably and properly, he can be executed. Beheading is customary for a noble; a gold sword, most acceptable. Shugdad would be the first to agree."

Lukas sat down. "I can't sack him. I can only kill him?"

"Execute," corrected Locman. "Precisely so."

Lukas said nothing, chewing over this news. Finally, he sighed, "All right. I'll deal with him some other way."

After telling Locman what had brought on this clash with the Vizier, Lukas asked for the Astrologer's own opinion.

"For one who studies the universe, the heavens, the grand movements of destiny written therein," replied Locman, "these earthly concerns are weightless, mere fleeting shadows."

"Yes," put in Lukas, "I thought you'd say so."

"On a lower plane," Locman continued, "as such things go in the palace, I can assure you there will be much talk; plans made and made again. A final war against

King Ardashir has been long brewing, even before the old King died. The Councillors and Commanders will agree, then disagree, then quarrel among themselves."

"Let them," said Lukas. "But what should I do?"

"What a king usually does," the Astrologer said. "Absolutely nothing."

CHAPTER

❦ 5 ❦

*A*s always, when given good advice, Lukas did the opposite. Next morning, to the astonishment of the Royal Valets and to his own, he got up well before noon. He had planned to spend his day first in the Royal Baths, then flying the Royal Falcons; and after that, attacking the knotty problem of what he might fancy for his dinner. Instead, he went straight to the one place he had shunned like the plague, the High Council Chamber.

There, only the gravest matters of state were discussed. Naturally, the Royal Ministers never expected him to set foot inside it. Shugdad, of course, was present. Lukas had been looking forward to seeing the Vizier explode with rage. Shugdad, however, welcomed him with every expression of joy and gratitude:

"Wonder of the Age, favor your servants with your perfect pearls of wisdom! Lighten the shadows of our ignorance! We hear and attend!"

A little taken aback by such warm greetings, Lukas began straightaway ordering the Council to end all plans to invade Bishangar. He commanded them to make a treaty with King Ardashir, to bargain for the treasure instead of taking it by storm. As he went on, he noticed some of the Councillors whispering behind their hands and smiling; others obviously stifled their yawns. When he finished, Shugdad, with great courtesy, questioned him on the nature of the treaty, on certain points of law, trade, and the state of the Royal Treasury. Not daring to admit he had no idea in the world what the Vizier was talking about, Lukas flushed and stammered whatever answers popped into his head. At last, he had to stop. Whereupon Shugdad thanked him for his brilliant discourse, prayed him to return at his pleasure to enlighten the Council, and bowed him out of the chamber.

"Damn Shugdad!" Lukas burst out when he was back in his apartments. "Damn that silk handkerchief! He made an ass of me!"

He stopped. "Worse than that. I made an ass of myself."

Still smarting, he had to face the unhappy fact that a king who spent his days feasting, splashing in the pool, blowing soap bubbles from the Royal Hookah, and otherwise entertaining himself, could hardly command serious attention. In any matter more important than deciding what color turban to wear, the Center of the Universe held as much sway as the Royal Carpet Spreader.

"And probably less," admitted Lukas. "Well, there's

more than one way to skin a cat. As for skinning a Grand Vizier, we'll soon find out."

Locman had foreseen disagreements among the Councillors. Lukas now set about proving the Astrologer correct. At home, Lukas had been quick to learn his letters, but had never burdened his head by reading a book. To him, the schoolhouse was the most dangerous place in town, a threat to life, limb, and brain.

But now, from the Royal Archivist, Lukas demanded volume after volume of laws, history, geography, arithmetic, and spent most of his days and nights poring over them. Hard thinking was one bad habit he had so far avoided.

"But I suppose it has to be done," he sighed. "It can't be worse than a case of colic."

His studies not only made his head ache, they interfered with his amusements. "This business of being King," he groaned. "Whoever imagined it had anything to do with ruling a kingdom!"

To his further dismay, he found he could not learn everything he needed to know in a few short days. Meanwhile, therefore, he resorted to what he did best: mischief and aggravation. From the Ministers he demanded reports and accountings. When these were presented, he declared them too wordy and sent them to be done over. Then he flung them back because they were too short.

"The Town Clerk," said Lukas, "would be proud of me."

Preparations for the war went ahead more slowly

every day. Yet there were moments when his spirits sank. One afternoon, he felt so gloomy that he asked the Court Astrologer for any heartening predictions.

"Of course, Meritorious One," said Locman. "I am able to reveal that all signs indicate you will enjoy a reign long, glorious, and triumphant."

"Good," said Lukas. "I only hope it's true."

"It must be," replied Locman. "The same is always predicted for every King of Abadan. When it turns out otherwise, the fault is the King's, not the prophecy's."

Lukas thanked him for such encouraging assurance. Nevertheless, by the end of the week he had proof that his efforts were succeeding magnificently. The Chief Scribe lost his temper and threw an ink horn at the Royal Magistrate; the Minister of War called the Commander of Guards a donkey; and all the Council, thanks to Lukas, were at loggerheads.

At the same time, his studies showed him something else. To his horror, he learned that even the least offenses carried terrible punishments: hands cut off, eyes gouged out—and these were the mildest penalties. He shuddered to think what his pranks at home would cost him here.

When he saw Locman again, he jabbed a finger at a volume of Royal Statutes. "Just look at this! It may be law, but there's devilish little justice in it."

"Center of the Universe," protested Locman, "these laws have been framed by the most upstanding and righteous of lawgivers: men of perfect virtue, unblemished character—"

"That's the trouble," said Lukas. "They aren't the ones who need the laws. Righteous, no doubt. But there're so few of them and so many of the other kind. No, this whole mess will have to be changed."

"If such is the King's will," said the Astrologer. "You need only command the Royal Prosecutor to draft new measures. He will submit his preliminary recommendations without delay. I should say, oh, in five or six years."

"What happens in the meantime?" cried Lukas. "Never mind. I'll have to do the work myself."

He clapped his hands to his head. "It's bad enough dealing with the Council, the Bishangaris. And now this! Whatever became of my holiday?"

He longed for the day when he could go back to the serious business of entertaining himself. The best he could manage was an occasional walk in the gardens. During one such, he strolled through a maze of shrubbery, farther than he had ventured before, enjoying his stolen moment of relaxation. He stopped short. Beyond a low stone wall was a small inner courtyard enclosed by an iron grille. In one corner, on a bench, sat Nur-Jehan.

Lukas hurried to the grille and called to her. At sight of him, Nur-Jehan started and jumped to her feet:

"What are you doing here? You cost me one beating. Are you determined, finally, to cost me my head?"

"Aren't these the Royal Gardens?" retorted Lukas. "If anybody has a right to walk in them—"

"These are the women's quarters. Even the King does not approach. You should not be here."

"Well, I am," said Lukas. "And since I am, you might be interested in something I can tell you."

"What could a King of Abadan say to me? His concerns are not mine, my concerns are not his."

"For one thing," said Lukas, "I wish you wouldn't talk at me as if I weren't here. For another, I'm not exactly the King of Abadan. Well, yes, in a way I am. But not as you might think. Sometimes I'm not even sure I'm myself. I mean, I know who I am, but something strange happened."

"The Kings of Abadan have been tyrants, warriors, and dotards. Now is the list to be completed by a fool?"

"I'm certainly a fool to talk to you if you won't listen," retorted Lukas. "You should be interested that I'm trying to save your head. Yours, Ardashir's, all the Bishangaris'."

Nur-Jehan, about to leave, halted and turned her face full on Lukas. "What do you know of King Ardashir?"

"Shugdad calls him a brigand, which makes me think Ardashir must be a decent sort of fellow. But that's not the point." Having gained the girl's attention, if not her good will, he told her the mischief he had worked in the Council, proudly adding, "Some of the Ministers are beginning to side with me. Shugdad isn't having it all his own way."

"Why does the King act on behalf of his enemy?"

"How do I know he's my enemy if I haven't tried making him a friend? Anyhow, the whole business is stupid. Both sides will end up killing each other. So don't think you're the only one concerned for the Bishangaris. The difference is when the King takes a hand in it, things get done."

"Then let the King do one thing more. Set me free. Or see that I am given a knife or a sword and I shall free myself."

"Well, you're a bloodthirsty creature, aren't you! I hope Ardashir has a better disposition. You haven't understood. These idiots are planning a massacre. The truth is, I'm not all that sure I can make them give it up, or how long I can hold it off. I'm not even sure how long I'll be here. But if Shugdad starts his war, Bishangar's the last place on earth anyone should want to be. Did you think you'd go and warn your King? Very noble, but you'd never get that far alone. And if Ardashir has any sense, he already expects an invasion. He doesn't need a village girl to tell him."

"It is not a question of warning. I wish to be among my own people."

"Also very noble," said Lukas, "and you'll end up nobly dead. You may be foolish enough to risk your neck. I won't help you at it. The best favor I can do is to keep you here. It's for your own good." Then, to himself, he added, "And where have I heard that before?"

"The King does not wish me to risk my neck," said Nur-Jehan. "Yet he seems willing to risk his own."

Lukas laughed. "How? Shugdad gnashing his teeth at me? Nahdir scowling me to death?"

"You truly are a fool," Nur-Jehan flung back, "and

certainly no king. How long will the Vizier suffer your games? Do you imagine you have Councillors on your side? Go too far, overstep yourself, they will not support you. You will see them cling to Shugdad, trembling for their heads, afraid the King will not be powerful enough to save them. Your efforts are in vain. If you insist on making them, beware. There may come a test of strength before you have strength to test."

A voice called from the women's quarters. Nur-Jehan broke off immediately, gestured Lukas away, and hurried through the arcade. He waited as long as he dared. She did not return.

He went back the following morning. Nur-Jehan was not there. He could stay only a few minutes, this being the day for the dispensation of justice. As in any matter of consequence, the Royal Presence was not required. However, in the midst of drafting new laws, he was eager to see things for himself. Therefore, Lukas hurried to the Divan of Judgment, where the day's business had already begun. Shugdad was in the forefront, with a gaggle of scribes and secretaries.

The culprit, hands roped behind his back, knelt in the middle of the hall. He was a lean, eagle-nosed, raffish fellow dressed in a ragbag of garments, which Lukas, by long familiarity, recognized as castoffs. His head was shaven smooth as the soles of his bare and grimy feet, but he sported an enormous, upturning, black moustache. The tips had once been twirled into points, but this vanity had come unstuck, leaving the ends as ragged as his sleeveless jacket.

The arrival of Lukas was attended by the usual ground-kissing on the part of the court officers, and by the Vizier's clenched reverences. Seating himself, Lukas demanded to know the nature of the case in hand.

"This one is called Kayim, O Master of the World," the Royal Secretary answered. "A street juggler, a public versifier, a thief, a gamester, a vagabond—"

"All at once?" asked Lukas. "Which is he accused of, thievery or bad verse?"

"Which is worse? To steal a purse?" Kayim glibly put in. "And who's the greater felon? The one to filch a melon? I judge the meaner crime's to skimp a rhyme."

At this, a guard cuffed the versifier on the head.

"Critic!" muttered Kayim, for which he was cuffed again.

The Grand Vizier turned to Lukas. "This is the most insolent rogue in Shirazan Bazaar. A worthless wretch, a worm, a nothing."

"If he's all that worthless," replied Lukas, "why bother with him?"

"He is guilty of high crimes against the King," declared Shugdad.

"Then he must have kept them very low. I'm sure I never noticed any."

"Not only against the King," said Shugdad, "but as well against the Grand Vizier and all the King's ministers."

The Royal Secretary assured Lukas this was the case, and read aloud from a parchment affirming that one Kayim, here detained thanks to the vigilance of Commander Nahdir, had willfully and maliciously recited one of his poems in the bazaar.

"Poem!" exclaimed Lukas. "I can see how it might be a punishment to read one. But to recite one?"

"The aforesaid poem slanders and defames all officers of the Royal Court," said the Secretary, "specifically Shugdad Mirza and the Center of the Universe himself."

Shugdad waved away the Secretary's indictment. "It comes to no less than high treason. The case is clear. The King need not waste his precious time in judgment."

"I've been defamed so often," said Lukas, "I'd like to hear if he's found anything new." Against the Vizier's protest, he ordered the prisoner to stand and repeat the verses.

"Let me think," said Kayim, fingering his shaven skull. "It was defamation, for the most part; with a touch of calumny and vilification to spice things up a little. If this is my last public performance, I want to get it right."

Clearing his throat, he began reciting an atrociously rhymed but comical poem about an unlucky fisherman. Twice he tried to pull in a fish, but each time a shark snapped it up. Finally he hooked a minnow, tried to stretch it to the size of a herring, and sell it to a foolish fishmonger. It was all outrageous nonsense, so cleverly turned that Lukas laughed until the tears rolled down his cheeks. He laughed still harder when it became clear that the minnow was the new King of Abadan; the Royal Ministers, the fishmonger; the shark, the Grand Vizier.

"Come on, Shugdad! What's the matter with you? It's the only good joke I've heard in the palace. Give him a purse of money and send him on his way."

Then he saw the look on the Vizier's face. Kayim's nonsense had struck a nerve. The doggerel, Lukas realized, strongly hinted that the other two prophesied monarchs had come to grief not accidentally.

"The King will condemn this villain to death," Shugdad said flatly. "First, let his tongue be torn out. Then he shall be impaled on a spear at the palace gate. The sentence is already written."

"Then unwrite it," said Lukas. "I didn't know you were so thin-skinned. If you condemn everybody who makes fun of you, that might depopulate the kingdom. No, he won't be punished."

"Mercy is a jewel on the King's hand when he forgives an insult to himself," declared Shugdad. "It is filth on the hem of his robe when he allows the honor of his ministers to be tainted."

Most of the Royal Councillors murmured agreement with the Vizier, among them a number Lukas had counted as siding with the King. He remembered Nur-Jehan's warning if he overstepped himself, if he went too far too soon. Shugdad, he realized, had chosen this moment for a test of strength. If Lukas forbade the sentence, the Ministers would close ranks against him. The life of a rogue, a foolish versifier—no sensible king would give it a second thought.

"Hear the King's judgment," said Lukas. "Set this Kayim free. Let him go unharmed."

No one spoke. The faces of the Councillors were closed and unreadable. He could not guess how many of them he had lost, or how much stronger the Vizier had grown. The guards, meantime, had unbound Kayim, who dropped to his knees before Lukas. The versifier's face paled and his moustache twitched desperately:

"O King," he murmured, "what have you done?"

"It seems to me," said Lukas, "that I saved your neck."

"Saved? For how long? Your Vizier wants my tongue and everything else. If he can't have them here, he'll send someone to collect them. I'll be a dead man before I set foot in Shirazan Bazaar."

"I see what you mean." Lukas sighed and shrugged. "I've gone this far, I might as well go the rest of the way."

He stood, looked over the dour faces of the Councillors, and announced:

"Hear the King. From this day, the versifier Kayim is first among servants of the Royal Household. He will have place in the Royal Chambers, under the King's protection, and he will answer only to the King."

With that, beckoning Kayim to follow, he strode out of the Divan of Judgment.

"Tell me," said Lukas as they were escorted back to

the Royal Apartments, "are you everything they said you were?"

"Oh, yes," Kayim answered brightly, "and much worse than they gave me credit for."

"Good," said Lukas. "You're the only one around here I can trust."

CHAPTER

6

*O*asis of Compassion in the Desert of Despair!"
cried Kayim, seeing his new chambers. "Fig Tree of
Abundance amid Thorns of Desolation! Shining Star
of—"

"Don't butter me," said Lukas. "Thanks to you, I'm
in a pickle already. But you gave me the only laugh I've
had in days. That poem—you may be a rogue, but you're
a bold one to recite it."

"Not recite it? Why, then, write it?" answered
Kayim. "The fox who has of jackals written, runs the
risk of being bitten. It was too amusing to keep to myself. Otherwise, I give you my word, I'm a most remarkable coward. And cowardice is a quality I recommend
highly, especially to the great and powerful, the better
part of wisdom, one of the noblest virtues. Believe me, O
King, if all were as cowardly as I am, what a marvelous
place the world would be."

Lukas grinned at him. "That's the first piece of common sense I've heard since I've been here. There's a Bishangari tiger who wants to hack her way out of the palace; the Court Astrologer's tangled up with comets and horoscopes. As for Shugdad, is it true that he did away with those other two would-be Kings?"

"Ah, well, there's true and there's true," said Kayim. "In the versifying sense, if I say a horse gallops like the wind—I've never seen the wind gallop, but it's true nevertheless. Who knows for certain about Shugdad? There's plenty of talk in the bazaar. They say he ordered them killed. I wouldn't put it past him."

"I wouldn't either," said Lukas. "But it doesn't make me feel very comfortable."

"Being a king's as risky as versifying," said Kayim, sprawling on the couch and propping up his feet. "All either of us can do—Oh, before I forget. Since I'm your servant, may the Cloak of Generosity enfold the Shoulders of Deprivation. I'll need some good clothes. Yes, as I was saying, all we can do is make the best of it."

"Kayim," said Lukas, "I'm sure you'll do exactly that."

Lukas was not wrong. Within the week, Kayim set the palace routines topsy-turvy. He wheedled special dainties from the cooks, badgered the tailors with fittings and refittings, poked and pried into every nook and cranny. He rummaged through Locman's charts and disputed all the Astrologer's predictions. He perfectly aped

Nahdir's voice and scowl, then dodged away, leaving him to lash at empty air. Kayim managed to avoid Shugdad altogether, prudent enough not to stretch his luck to breaking.

The versifier was never on hand when Lukas wanted him. When he was, Kayim busied himself curling his moustache, picking his teeth with the Royal Dagger, or oiling his shaven scalp until it gleamed. Coming back from his Council meetings or the Royal Archives at the end of the day, Lukas would find Kayim still at breakfast, sprawled on the cushions amid orange peels and melon rinds.

"You're a worse rascal than I am," Lukas told him. "I crack my skull over laws and decrees—and I'm supposed to be King! If there's loafing to be done, I should be the one to do it."

Kayim, nevertheless, with his preposterous tales and outrageous doggerel, was the only one who could make him laugh. And only to Kayim did Lukas confide how he had come to Abadan.

The versifier assured Lukas he had heard of stranger doings. "Or so the tales go, whether they happened or didn't happen. Princes made beggars, beggars made princes, or sent flying away on wooden horses. You could have done worse. This Battisto at least made you a king. He could as easily have set you to sweeping streets or tending camels."

"Sometimes I wonder if there was ever such a person," said Lukas. "What if I'd always been here? Was I only dreaming of a place called Zara-Petra? Or am I only dreaming of a place called Abadan?"

"*You* may be dreaming," said Kayim. "*I'm* not. That little entertainment Shugdad had in mind for me would have been real enough. But I don't worry too much about it any more. If I so much as sniff 'impalement' in the wind, it's out your secret passage with me!"

"What passage? What are you talking about?"

"The tunnel under the palace wall, what else?"

"Idiot!" burst out Lukas. "Why didn't you tell me about it before?"

"I thought you knew. It's your palace, isn't it?" With that, Kayim explained that one morning an apricot had fallen out of his hand and rolled into a corner. Picking up the fruit, he had accidentally pressed one of the tiles. He pointed to the spot. "See, the pattern's different. Go on, push."

Lukas did so, and before his eyes a narrow section of wall swung silently inward. "You've gone through it? Outside the palace?"

"Three or four times. Did you think I'd stay cooped up here all day?"

Eager for the sights and smells of the bazaar, Lukas would have plunged through the doorway then and there. Kayim pulled him back:

"The King in his finery? What a sight in Shirazan Bazaar!"

"Call the Royal Tailors. They can stitch up some rags."

"No need." Kayim pulled a bundle from under the couch. "Here. These will do."

"You had them ready?"

"I merely anticipated," said Kayim, winking, "that someday you'd enjoy a little anonymous outing."

Lukas pulled off his garments as fast as he could and dressed himself in the tatters. While the versifier changed his own costume, Lukas called through the door to Osman, his bodyguard, and ordered him to let no one enter the chambers or disturb the King for any reason.

"Come on," said Lukas. "We'll be back before anyone knows I've been gone."

With Kayim leading, the two scuttled down a low-ceilinged, unlighted tunnel. Lukas groped his way along damp walls of masonry. Just when his lungs began laboring for want of air, he glimpsed a pale glow some distance ahead. Kayim hurried on. By the time Lukas caught up with him, the versifier had produced a thin metal rod, hooked at one end, and was busy picking the lock of an iron wicket. In a moment, the gate creaked open. Blinking in the late afternoon sunlight, Lukas found himself in a grove of trees and shrubbery. They hurried across, into a twisting alleyway. The next turn brought them to the middle of Shirazan Bazaar.

Jostling through the crowd, Lukas happily put aside all thoughts of Shugdad, Council meetings, and new laws. Excited, he wanted to see everything at once. Kayim, however, urged him to go first to the Caravanserai of the Sun and Moon, which Lukas guessed to be a kind of inn. The versifier was on good terms there with a man called Saalab, whose trade was leading merchants and travelers to outlying cities. From him, Lukas could hear the latest gossip.

"Better than the news you get in Shirazan Palace," Kayim said, "after the Vizier and Royal Ministers finish scrubbing and perfuming it. What Saalab tells you might have a certain aroma of camel, but you can believe most of it. He'll never know you for the King, so he'll be honest with you."

Lukas agreed, but as Kayim led him through the bazaar he hung back and stopped by a fruit seller's booth. A basket of ripe figs had caught his eye and appetite, but the versifier reminded him:

"They don't sell on credit here. Unless you brought money, you'll have to do without. Of course, if you'll wink at some straightforward thievery, I'll filch us a couple of handfuls."

"No need," said Lukas. "I'll send the money later. Right now, let me have a little fun. It will make me feel at home again."

With that, he stepped up to the counter. Instead of asking for figs, he made a show of looking over all the other fruit. Finally, he said:

"Let's have two of those oranges, master fruit seller, if you're sure they're ripe."

"Ripe enough for a bazaar loafer," answered the fruit seller. He set the oranges on the counter and held out a hand for payment.

"Wait a minute," said Lukas. "I've changed my mind. Those figs will suit my taste better. A sackful, if you please, and I'll thank you not to slip in any moldy ones."

Declaring that neither he, nor his father, nor his grandfather had ever sold a bad fig—which, Lukas saw, did not keep him from including a number of suspicious-looking ones—the vendor filled a small sack. As Lukas was about to walk off with it, the fruit seller snatched it away:

"Destroyer of profits!" he cried. "Scrofulous Camel in the Tent of Prosperity! Where's the money? Let's have that first."

Lukas gave him a puzzled but patient look. "Why, master, what a curious thing to say. As I didn't want the oranges, I traded them for these figs."

"So you did," the fruit seller admitted. "But do you think my memory's as ragged as yours? You never paid me for the oranges."

"Of course I didn't," said Lukas.

"Oho! You admit it!"

"For a very good reason," said Lukas, pretending vexation. "I didn't take them."

"What's that?" cried the fruit seller. "Didn't take them?"

"There you see them on your counter," said Lukas. "Now, let's have the figs and I won't call down the law on you for trying to swindle a poor orphaned innocent."

The fruit vendor stared from the figs to the oranges and back again, scratching his head and counting on his fingers:

"Hold on, there. Something doesn't come out right."

"I don't see that." Lukas shrugged. "You've got your oranges, I've got my figs."

Befuddled though he was, the fruit vendor locked his mind onto one clear fact: He was losing both fee and fruit.

"Twister of Thought!" he cried. "Fig stealer!"

Snatching a long stick, he came storming from behind his counter. So taken aback at his scheme blowing up in his face, Lukas could scarcely collect his wits before the fruit vendor lit into him, whacking him about the head and shoulders, bellowing at the top of his voice. The versifier tried to pull Lukas free of the indignant fruit seller, but onlookers gathered so quickly he was jostled away from his unlucky friend.

A rap from the vendor's stick set Lukas's nose bleeding. Kayim had been lost in the crowd. The fruit seller bawled for the constables. A few moments more, Lukas feared, and the King of Abadan would be tossed into one of his own lockups.

Spying an opening in the crowd, Lukas darted through. He saw nothing of the versifier. Certain Kayim had made good his escape, Lukas dashed from the bazaar, dodging, doubling his tracks, at last leaving the furious merchant far behind.

Once out of danger, Lukas sat down by an angle of wall. His taste for figs had vanished. He turned his attention to stanching his bleeding nose.

"There's a fine sight. Did you buy that nose in the bazaar? Or did someone give it to you for nothing?"

Looking down on him was a stocky, stubby-legged man whose garments were even more tattered than those of Lukas. On his balding head was a pointed skullcap of felt; from his shoulder hung a goatskin with a brass faucet at one end. His face was broad and leathery, rough-bearded as the water bag he carried; but he grinned good-naturedly as he started filling a cup attached to a long chain.

Lukas felt dry enough to swallow the vendor's whole stock in one gulp; but, having run afoul of one merchant, he was reluctant to have another painful misunderstanding.

"I'd better tell you straight out," said Lukas, "I don't have any money."

"Who asked?" replied the water seller. "You look like you've had a bad day. It couldn't be worse than mine. I've hardly sold a drop. My bag's heavier than when I started out this morning. Go on, drink up. Only don't think I make a habit of this." Despite his grumbling, the water seller filled the cup again as soon as Lukas had gratefully downed the first.

"I'll pay you back," said Lukas, "I promise. Meantime, I'll tell you this: King Kasha himself couldn't have a royal thirst like mine."

"King Kasha? He's welcome to a drink from Namash any time he wants it."

"I'll be sure to tell him," said Lukas, "next time I see him. So, you think well of him?"

"I do," said Namash, "and I'm not the only one. There's plenty of folk in Shirazan Bazaar to wish him well. From what I hear, he's a good sort—for a king. I say Long life to King Kasha!"

"I couldn't agree with you more," said Lukas.

Thanking the water seller, he set off to find Kayim.

Luckily, he had not gone far when he caught sight of the versifier at the end of a street leading from the bazaar. Kayim ran to meet him and, after making sure Lukas had suffered more in his pride than his person, the versifier laughed and shook his head:

"The Staff of Righteousness has fallen on the Nose of Iniquity. Come on, we'll gossip with Saalab tomorrow. It's late and you've stirred up enough trouble already."

"I don't know what went wrong," said Lukas. "Back home, the trick never failed."

"Being King may have spoiled you for a rascal," said Kayim. "I hope not. There's no lack of rogues, in or out of palaces; but a good-hearted one—that's not easy to find."

"Namash is to be given a bag of gold pieces," said Lukas, as they hurried through the gathering dusk. "But I don't want him to know where it comes from or who sends it."

"That's a nice price for a drink of water," said Kayim.

"I'd quit versifying and go into that trade myself if I could count on such generous customers."

"It's for more than water," said Lukas. He told the versifier what had happened. By the time he finished, they had entered the grove outside the palace wall.

Kayim halted a moment to bend down and shake a pebble from his shoe. As he did, something hissed through the air. Lukas fell back and cried a warning.

In the trunk of a tree quivered a dagger.

CHAPTER

❧❧ 7 ❧❧

*B*ehind them, a figure sprang from the shadows. Lukas could make out nothing of the attacker's face; nor, at the moment, was he interested in doing so. With one mind, the pair took to their heels. The versifier, as glib with his feet as he was with his rhymes, raced beside Lukas, and both plunged headlong through the gate. Kayim slammed it shut, hastily locked it, and the two never stopped running until they were once more in the Royal Chambers.

Even in the safety of the King's quarters, Kayim took some while to regain his calm. He paced up and down, frowning, cracking his knuckles, too unsettled to repair his frayed moustache.

"I never thought my critics would go that far," he muttered. "A public versifier's bound to offend somebody. A hazard of the trade. But a knife in the ribs? No, it's not my verses, it's your Vizier. Shugdad's in this. He swore he'd have my tongue. He'll settle for my neck."

"Yes, it has to be Shugdad's work," said Lukas, still shaken as he thought of the dagger in the tree. "Was that knife meant only for you? You've been watched. Somebody knew you found a way out of the palace."

"True, but whoever it was couldn't have guessed you'd be with me."

"Then it was a lucky, or unlucky, chance. Two birds with one stone. Shugdad wants to get rid of you, but don't forget the shark and the minnow. He'd be still happier to get rid of me."

"Much as I find the idea personally distasteful," said Kayim, "you'd have been wiser if you'd handed me over to him in the first place."

"If killing is one of the royal duties," answered Lukas, "to the devil with it. That Bishangari told me I was no king. She was right. Shugdad will do what he wants and I can't stop him. You'd be safer anywhere but Shirazan."

"Are you telling me to escape and leave you here? I owe you my life, not to mention a fine suit of clothes. Neither comes easy in my line of work. I admit being a coward, but not a thankless one."

"We'll both get out of this hornet's nest," said Lukas. "I don't know much about ruling a kingdom, but I know when to pack up. Right away. It's the last thing Shugdad will expect."

"I agree," said Kayim, "but it galls me. The King of Abadan sneaking off—"

"Not sneaking," said Lukas. "Running proudly. The game's over. I'm not ashamed to admit it. I'd be a fool if I waited for Shugdad to try again."

"Good," said Kayim. "Off we go."

"Not quite yet. I should have let the Bishangari girl escape when she asked me. Now she'll have to come with us."

Kayim clapped his hands to his head. "Has the Lamp of Reason spilled the Oil of Intelligence into the Dust of Stupidity? Talk about Shugdad! Any Bishangari would be delighted to finish his work."

"I'll take that chance. I'm not leaving till she's freed."

Kayim sighed. "Very well. Stay here and let me see what I can do."

Explaining no further, the versifier hurried from the Royal Chambers.

One task remained for Lukas. He ordered Osman, the guard on duty at his door, to send for the Astrologer. He put on a cloak to hide the rags he still wore. When Locman arrived, Lukas commanded him to have a purse of gold put secretly into the hands of the water seller.

"It shall be done this very hour without fail," said Locman. "But may I ask why?"

"No. Just make certain of it. And Locman, have you seen anything upsetting in your horoscopes?"

"Not the slightest. On the contrary, every portent indicates peace, happiness, and utmost tranquility."

"That's what worries me." Nevertheless, he thanked Locman and dismissed him sadly. Despite his less than reliable predictions, the Astrologer meant no harm.

"Which is more than I can say for Battisto," Lukas told himself. "I thought he was doing me a favor. Grand holiday? Grand mess! For all I know, this whole business may be out of his hands. There may be nothing he can do about it now. Or is he doing it on purpose? Is it my fault? Did I somehow rub him the wrong way?"

Finding no sensible answer, he could only force himself to be patient. As the hours passed, however, he grew more and more uneasy. He had no idea what the versifier planned. Kayim, at this very moment, might be captured or even dead; Nur-Jehan, too. He wondered how much longer he dared wait. If Kayim and the girl did not come soon, he would have to risk leaving the chamber and searching for them.

At last, there was a rap at the door. Lukas jumped to his feet. Instead of the versifier, the guard Osman entered:

"Center of the Universe, I bear a message from the Grand Vizier."

"Tell Shugdad the King takes his rest and will hear nothing from him." Lukas spoke as calmly as he could, even as he cursed himself for not having sent Osman away. Kayim, if he succeeded, would still have to bring the girl past the guard's watchful eye. Hastily, Lukas added, "Go to the Vizier yourself. Say that I'll speak with him at noon. It's nearly dawn, the new guard will be here soon, so you needn't come back. If anyone questions you, tell him it's the King's command."

"Forgive me, O King," replied Osman. "I must obey my orders."

"Obey, then," snapped Lukas. "I told you—"

He stopped short. From the sash at his waist, Osman had taken a bowstring. As Lukas suddenly realized its purpose, the guard stepped forward and in a quick motion looped the cord around his neck.

Lukas had not a moment to cry out as the bowstring bit into his throat. He clawed at the cord, kicked and fought to wrestle free. Osman, taller and better muscled than Lukas, steadily tightened the noose. Eyes starting from his head, Lukas felt his strength ebbing. Only the grip of Osman kept him from falling.

Lights shattered in his head. He seemed to see Nur-Jehan with another woman beside her. The girl was raising her clasped hands, bringing them down as if she were swinging an ax. Osman grunted. The bowstring went slack.

Lukas dropped to the floor and threw himself clear of the staggering guard.

"The bowstring!" cried Nur-Jehan. "Get it. Quickly!"

Lukas, bewildered, only stared at her. With a cry of impatience, Nur-Jehan snatched up the cord herself. With a strength Lukas had never suspected, she forced Osman's arms behind him, set a knee in the guard's back, and hastily bound his wrists; then she undid the man's sash and gagged him with it.

To his added bewilderment, Lukas saw the girl's companion tear away her skirts, pull the veil from her face, and peel off her scalp. Head glistening, moustache waving, Kayim grinned at him.

"Here's your Bishangari," said the versifier, as Nur-Jehan turned to bolt the door. "It took longer than I thought. But I see you've had company to entertain you.

"I'm sorry for your inconvenience," Kayim went on. "We'd have been here hours ago if the Royal Slave Mistress hadn't taken forever to go to sleep. She has terrible insomnia. I had to wait to steal her clothes. She won't be pleased when she wakes up and finds her best silks missing. Did you know she wears a wig? Lucky—for me, that is. As for the rest, what could be more natural than a court lady chivying a slave girl? We strolled out of the women's quarters as nicely as you please. I can guess what was happening here."

Nur-Jehan pointed angrily. "This versifier is a fool. Had he been found out, we should both have been killed on the spot. Why has he brought me here? He only babbled something about a plot. This has nothing to do with me."

"It has a lot to do with you," returned Lukas. "Kayim and I could have been out of here long ago. You wanted to be set free. I thought I'd oblige you."

"Free, not caught in a trap," retorted the girl. "The whole palace will be up in arms to storm this chamber. It is too late to correct your stupidity. Are there weapons here? I mean to sell my life dearly."

"I don't mean to sell mine at any price," said Lukas. "So don't start going on about standing off the palace guards, Shugdad, and all the rest."

"I am a Bishangari. When our backs are to the wall—"

"When your back's to the wall," said Lukas, "the best thing is to go through it." He showed Nur-Jehan the passageway. "We'll take you with us. It's your only chance. Unless you'd rather stay behind and valiantly fling sofa cushions."

Nur-Jehan bit her lips. She nodded a curt agreement. Lukas picked up his dagger. Unsheathing it, he crouched beside Osman and set the point against the guard's throat:

"Listen to me carefully, Osman. I'm taking off that gag. But, one peep above a whisper—you understand me?"

Osman bowed his head. As Lukas undid the sash, the guard murmured, "Take my life, Center of the Universe, but I swear to you, I did only as Shugdad Mirza commanded."

"I'm sure you did," replied Lukas, "but since when is Shugdad King of Abadan?"

"On word of your death, he will name himself King. The Royal Ministers will acclaim him."

"Did Locman know anything of this?"

"Nothing. He was not consulted. The matter was agreed between the Vizier and the Commander of Guards."

"For my own satisfaction," put in Kayim, "since I always like to be familiar with people interested in killing me, who was hiding outside the wall?"

"Nahdir Aga. When he learned that you and the King had gone to the bazaar, he thought it simpler if neither of you returned alive to the palace."

Lukas pressed the dagger more firmly. "Is the passageway still watched? The truth, Osman."

"It is not. There was no further need to guard it. Nahdir failed, but that was of no importance. Since the King had come back to his chambers, I was to strangle him here."

"Yes," muttered Kayim, "and me along with him."

"No," replied Osman. "The servant of the King was to be taken alive, then impaled. So Shugdad vowed to do."

The versifier swallowed hard and wiped his brow. "The Vizier's a man of his word. Let's be gone, Wonder of the Age, before he keeps it."

Lukas replaced the gag while Kayim trussed Osman's legs and made certain all bonds were secure. Nur-Jehan frowned at Lukas:

"Surely the King does not mean to let this traitor live?"

"Surely the King does."

"What, is the King's hand too delicate?" Nur-Jehan's eyes flashed. "Here, give me the knife."

Before Nur-Jehan could seize the dagger, Lukas tucked it under the folds of his shirt. "Let him be. There's nothing to gain from killing him. Besides, I'm not one to hold a grudge. Not even against hotheaded Bishangaris."

The versifier was frantically gesturing for them to join him in the passageway. Nur-Jehan looked scornfully at Lukas, then stepped through the opening. Lukas followed; this time, however, with spirits lower than before.

Osman had not lied. The gate was unguarded and they entered the grove safely. The sun had begun to rise and Kayim urged them to a faster pace. Lukas hesitated for one backward glance. The domes and spires of Shirazan Palace shone gold and crimson. In the early light, the traceries of stone shimmered weightless as a spider's web.

"For a while, Battisto had me living like a king," Lukas murmured as he hurried to catch up with the two shadows ahead of him. "The ridiculous part was that I started wanting to be a good one."

CHAPTER

❈ *8* ❈

*H*e expected Kayim to make straight for Shirazan
Bazaar, where they could lose themselves in the rabbit
warren of shops, arcades, and courtyards. Instead, the
versifier bent his steps in the opposite direction, through
streets empty and silent in the haze, to a seldom-used
gate. Avoiding the drowsy watchmen, they clambered
one by one through a loophole in the wall, and from there
darted into a stretch of untended, overgrown fields. They
followed a stream winding among grassy hillocks, at last
reaching a dell where Kayim halted.

"The bazaar's the first place they'll think of," said
Kayim, answering Lukas's unspoken question. "Shugdad
will ransack every stall, every house if he has to. I have
an idea. But first, I'm going to the bazaar by myself. This
stream runs into a drain under the wall. I've used it before, as the occasion required. I can be there and back in
no time, as soon as I find out what's what."

Nur-Jehan had crouched down a little apart from them. Lukas was about to join her when the versifier continued, "I have one unhappy task. This moustache must be eliminated. My hirsute appendage is too well known. I hate to see it go: Joy of my Heart, Adornment of my Upper Lip, Faithful Companion to my Nose. However, better to lose a moustache than the whole head. No one, of course, thought to bring a razor."

Lukas remembered his dagger and handed it to Kayim. Using the stream for a barber's mirror, and heaving rueful sighs, the versifier began hacking away. In a little while, he was more or less shorn. Since he had been unable to shave closely, clumps of bristles remained, spiking off in all directions. The absence of his moustache made him look more raffish than its presence. Even so, Lukas agreed he was much less recognizable.

"Keep this," Kayim said, tossing Lukas the dagger. "It's the only weapon among us, and you might need it. I'll bring back what news I can. Some food, too. I don't like being hunted on an empty stomach."

The versifier set off toward Shirazan. Lukas sat down beside Nur-Jehan. "I don't know what he has in mind, but he's bound to come up with something."

"If we ever see him again," said the girl, adding scornfully, "The word of an Abadani is woven of wind."

"Kayim admires you, too." Lukas grinned at her. "I'm sure he trusts you every bit as far as you trust him."

"He need not trouble himself," said Nur-Jehan. "Nor need you. With or without your help, I shall make my way to Bishangar. Had you let me go when I asked, I should have done it more safely. Now there will be troops in the countryside."

"Shugdad's after me, not you. He's not going to waste time on a girl from the wilds of Bishangar. He has bigger fish to fry. He wants the whole province, not a runaway slave. Do you know why? I wouldn't expect so. But I can tell you what's behind the whole thing: gold, silver, gems—"

"The King will teach me about Bishangar? That is no secret. Every hill child knows where veins of ore and precious stones can be found."

"According to Shugdad," said Lukas, with deliberate mischief, "the Bishangaris have no idea what they're walking on."

"An ass looks in the mirror and sees a wise Abadani. Truly, do you take us for such fools?"

"In that case, if there's so much wealth, why doesn't your King Ardashir dig it out? Trade with it. That's only common sense. Bishangar could be the richest country in the world."

"You have been ill-instructed in our history," said Nur-Jehan, "if you have been instructed at all."

"The books in the Royal Archives—"

"Written by Abadanis."

"Then let's hear your side of it."

"Does the King know that Bishangar was once a happy and prosperous kingdom?" said Nur-Jehan. "This is true. Long ago, in the days of King Neriman, we traded our metals and jewels for grain and foodstuffs from Abadan. Though rich in gold and silver, our land was poor in one thing even more precious: water. The mountain freshets were not enough for our needs; the lowlands were parched, little could be grown there, while Abadan had abundant harvests.

"Both kingdoms thrived and were at peace. King Neriman built the great city, Jannat al-Khuld, on the plain of Bishangar, gateway to the mountains. In that age, Jannat rose mighty as Shirazan and more beautiful.

"King Neriman died and his daughter, Tamina, became Queen; for it is our custom, unlike the Abadani, to honor queens as highly as kings. It was then that Afrasyab, ruler of Abadan, his heart eaten by greed, sought to increase his treasure.

"Afrasyab commanded that henceforth Bishangar would pay double the price in gold and silver for all goods bought from Abadan. Queen Tamina at first protested, but accepted for the sake of her people. Again, Afrasyab doubled the price. Again, though unwilling, Queen Tamina accepted.

"At this, the King's greed only sharpened. Soon he demanded a price threefold, then fourfold greater. At last, Queen Tamina refused. Ores were still plentiful in the earth, and Tamina knew that in reasonable quantity they could be mined without destruction to the land. But Afrasyab's greed, if satisfied, would have turned the country into a desolation of pits, mine shafts, and smelteries; and the Bishangaris no more than drudges toiling for Abadan. Queen Tamina's people saw this danger as clearly as she did, and stood with her in all heart and strength.

"Afrasyab then sent armies against Bishangar to force his will upon us. The Bishangaris fought bravely. Many gave their lives, as Queen Tamina gave hers. Yet, Jannat fell to Abadan. Afrasyab plundered it and claimed all Bishangar a province of his kingdom. It was a province in name only. My people, with the Queen's son, withdrew into the Mountains of Ramayan, where every crag became a fortress for them. So it has been ever since."

"What of King Ardashir?" asked Lukas. "I wanted to bargain with him. Why won't Shugdad do the same? Surely they could come to some agreement."

"Shugdad will never come to any agreement. He fears Ardashir too much. Ardashir has been our greatest King since Neriman, though his kingdom is now one of harsh mountains and his army a scattering of what the Abadanis call brigands. He longs for peace and fights only to defend himself. But he makes his own plans as well. Once his preparations are complete, his mountain cavalry could retake Jannat. Shugdad knows this; and, fearing Ardashir as he does, he has held back from an invasion in strength. But now he must invade, for Ardashir's forces have grown to readiness. If the Council delays, it is because they are reluctant to risk war against a king greater than any ruler of Abadan."

"Greater than King Kasha, that's for sure," put in

Lukas. "So, Shugdad's afraid to fight Ardashir, but thinks he has to fight him anyway. No one ever told me anything of that."

"Do royal ministers tell truth to kings? Have the Kings of Abadan desired truth?"

"And the Council," Lukas went on, "they'd have done the same, whether I was there or not. What you're telling me is I made a fool of myself. Nothing I did could have made any difference. For all it mattered, I could as well have spent my time flying kites. Idiot! I really thought I could rule a kingdom. And ended up with a bowstring around my neck."

"I warned you. You would not listen."

"True," Lukas admitted glumly. "Well, to the devil with all of them. Being a king isn't my line of work. The best I can do now, I suppose, is hole up somewhere and hope Shugdad never finds me. But where? Certainly not Bishangar. And if you still mean to go there, you're a bigger fool than I am."

"You speak without knowledge," said Nur-Jehan. "In that, you have become very much an Abadani. I have my own reason."

"Then tell me."

During her account of King Ardashir, Nur-Jehan had seemed more open and forthcoming than Lukas had ever seen her. Now, at his last words, she turned her eyes away and drew back into herself.

"I cannot."

"You mean you won't," said Lukas. "If it's all that important, I'd better know about it."

"It is important only to me," said Nur-Jehan. "To you, it will mean nothing."

"You can let me judge that," said Lukas. Nur-Jehan did not reply. He plucked at the grass. This girl with her bony face and yellow cat's eyes had a remarkable gift for aggravating him. "Never mind. Keep your little secret. I can guess. It's some village fellow, goatherd or some such."

Color spread across the ridge of her cheekbones. Lukas chuckled. The girl was actually blushing, as much as possible under the dark mottling of weathered skin.

"That is not so," she retorted. "And if it were?"

"Then I don't understand."

"You do not need to understand." Nur-Jehan stood and moved farther down the stream. Lukas sat by the water's edge. Neither spoke again.

Thus Kayim found them.

"Aha!" cried the versifier. "I see you've grown to be close and happy friends."

Lukas jumped to his feet, as impatient to hear Kayim's news as he was relieved to see him back safely. The versifier made a face:

"Things could be worse. That's to say, they could be a lot better. Shugdad hasn't proclaimed himself King. Not yet, in any case. There's no rumor that you're missing. But, one way or another, the Magpie of Gossip will flee the Snare of Silence. Some servant in the palace will blab, and they'll soon hear of it in the bazaar. For the moment, Shugdad may be trying to keep it quiet. But he can't sit on that kind of news very long."

"That's good, then," said Lukas.

"No, that's bad. Nahdir's men are combing the city. They're not calling attention to themselves, but they're watching everything that moves. That's why I took so long getting back."

Lukas shook his head. "That's bad."

"No, that's good. They still think we're in Shirazan. By the time they realize we aren't, we'll be somewhere else. The best thing, if you ask me, is to join a caravan, one of the big ones. We can lose ourselves in it. With so many travelers, who'd notice three more? My friend Saalab, the caravan leader, would take us along, no questions asked. So I went to the Sun and Moon—"

"I knew you'd come up with a plan! That's perfect!"

"No, that's bad. The caravan left already. Saalab set out at dawn, heading for Turan. We're too late. There won't be another for weeks."

"That's bad."

"You're right this time," said Kayim. "It's very bad."

"We're stuck, then," groaned Lukas. "If only we'd gone straight to Saalab, we'd be well on our way now. What smarts worst of all is that we missed it by so little."

"I doubt we can catch up with it." Kayim plucked at the stubble where his moustache once had flourished.

"Saalab has too much of a start on us. Though it might be worth a try. He'll follow the caravan trail along the River Hazra. If we do the same, and keep moving as fast as we can—"

"If you do the same," put in Nur-Jehan, who had come to listen to Kayim's account, "you will be taken by Nahdir. Do you think he will search only the bazaar? His troops will spread over the countryside. It is truly said, the Abadani digs a pit and falls into it backwards."

"Yes," Kayim returned, "and it's also said, the Bishangari sees a shovel and wonders how to put a saddle on it."

"You're a delightful critic," Lukas told the girl. "Of course, you have something better to suggest. If you don't think we should join the caravan, then what?"

"I did not say that. The Abadani is right, as far as the caravan is concerned. We can reach it safely, and sooner, if we take a different way. The caravan follows the Hazra. But we strike overland through the mountains. The Pass of Thaniyyat al-Ukab opens near the east bank of the river, well before Turan."

"What, go breaking our necks in the mountains?" cried Kayim. "I'm not a Bishangari goat!"

"True," said Nur-Jehan. "You have not that distinction."

"Never mind all that," said Lukas. "Are you sure this Thaniyyat al-Whatever will bring us out where we want? Won't Nahdir's men search the mountains, too?"

"Even if they do," answered Nur-Jehan, "we can

travel faster. There is better cover than in the flatlands. It is the way I meant to follow when I first escaped."

"All right," said Lukas. Though still resenting the girl's keeping so closemouthed about some nonsensical secret, he grudgingly added, "Will you lead us?"

"Will you follow a Bishangari?"

Lukas nodded. Kayim, sighing bleakly, reached into his garments and pulled out a few strings of dried figs and some pieces of withered fruit, along with a leather water flask:

"This is the best I could do, with Nahdir's guards breathing down my neck. Yes, I might as well go along with you. Scrambling over mountains—as a public versifier, I'd rather rhyme than climb. But let's get on with it. If verses were curses, or curses were verses, either way, I could end up with the longest epic of my short career."

CHAPTER
✖ 9 ✖

The girl strode out swiftly on her long legs, and set such a pace that Lukas and the versifier were hard-pressed to keep up with her.

"She's showing off," Lukas muttered to Kayim. "She'll get tired in a little while."

Nur-Jehan, however, did not slacken. Lukas soon found it more and more difficult to lift his heavy feet; with each new blister, he admitted, in rueful admiration, that she was tougher and more determined than he had ever supposed.

Bearing a little southward, they forded the Hazra and from there began their ascent into the hills. The slopes were densely wooded, but the overgrowth did not hamper the girl's progress. She had plaited her hair into one long tress and bound it around her head to avoid snagging it on low-hanging branches. She clambered lightly over the sharp ridges, her head thrown back, eyes watchful. In the cooler air of the heights, she seemed changed into a creature altogether different.

"Yes," grumbled Kayim when Lukas remarked on this. "Half cat and half goat. Between the two, they'll ruin me for life. Let her go on by herself. I'll find a comfortable cave and take up the hermit's trade instead of versifying. Then, at least, I can sit down for a few years."

The girl ignored these lamentations. When Lukas or Kayim showed signs of wearying, she resorted to such a combination of tongue-lashing and browbeating that they pressed on out of sheer vexation. If the luckless Kayim went sprawling over a root and vowed never to move again, the girl's tart words brought him to his feet. She scornfully challenged Lukas to match her in a dangerous leap from an outcropping of rocks. To his astonishment, Lukas did so. As the day drew to its end, Lukas began to suspect it was her will and not his own that drove them.

"I should have treated my Councillors like that," he admitted to Kayim. "Shugdad, too. I'd have had them jumping through hoops. She's a stringy, prickly, hot-blooded village vixen—but, I swear, she could have ruled the kingdom better than I did."

At nightfall, the girl allowed them to rest, and grudgingly told them they had made better progress than she had hoped.

"Do you hear that?" exclaimed Lukas. "Can it be a compliment? It halfway sounded like one. And look! Remarkable! I'd call that something of a smile. Not large, mind you, but I did notice a twitch. Or was it a flicker? Ah, too bad, it's gone."

Kayim had already stretched out below a narrow shelf of rock, his groans changing quickly to snores. At Lukas's banter, the girl had turned away.

"I advise the King to sleep as well as he can," she said in her customary tone, "even if there are no couches and carpets for his ease."

"I don't know how I'll manage without them," said Lukas, in mock dismay. "At home, in my own kingdom, I slept in all the comforts of doorways, with a marvelous quilt of flour sacks. Sometimes in a barrel, empty of course. My favorite bed was a regal heap of wood shavings."

Seeing Nur-Jehan's questioning frown, he laughed. "Oh, come on, girl, what did you take me for? Some princeling born and bred? My real name's Lukas, and before I crawled out of the ocean I lived in a town—don't ask me where it is now, because I don't know. I hadn't a penny to my name. Well, yes, I had one, but I spent it. On the other hand, I was a master of my trade."

"What trade was that?"

"Official Ne'er-Do-Well. There has to be one, you know. Just as there has to be, say, the village idiot or the town drunkard. Otherwise, how can respectable folk know how respectable they are? The Mayor swore I'd come to a bad end. That was the only intelligent thing he ever said."

"You did nothing? You cared for nothing?" The girl looked at him with solemn eyes. "You are joking."

"With you? Heaven forbid! If it hadn't been for a bungler called Battisto, I'd still be there, and better off than I am now." He told her what the mountebank had done.

Instead of the scornful reply he expected, Nur-Jehan said thoughtfully, "Then you were sent here against your will? And this man, Battisto, could bring you back at any instant? That is a frightening way to live."

"I'm trying to get used to it," said Lukas. "Yes, it's a little unsettling, not knowing if he'll snatch me away or leave me here forever. But no worse, I suppose, than anything else."

"Yet you risked your life for the sake of Bishangar, a land that can mean nothing to you."

"I tried to do some good for Abadan, too," said Lukas. "That was a big mistake. I should have let well enough alone. Don't ask how I got mixed up in law books and archives. One thing led to another, and there I was, tangled worse than flypaper. Had I known it was going to be so much work, not to mention getting strangled, I'd have kept on amusing myself royally. Still, I couldn't resist. Believe me, though, I'd rather sail a kite than rule a kingdom. I hope I've convinced you that I'm happily, proudly worthless."

"Our village wisewomen tell this tale," said Nur-Jehan. "Once, King Neriman's councillors asked him to decide which of two warriors was the more courageous.

Both did deeds of equal valor. But the first had the heart of a lion, bold and undaunted; while the heart of the second was filled always with dread, and fearful as a mouse.

" 'Surely, O King,' said the councillors, 'you must choose the first, for he is brave by his very nature; whereas the other is obliged to force bravery on himself.'

" 'This is true,' said Neriman. 'Therefore, I choose the second.'

"Sleep now, Lukas-Kasha," said Nur-Jehan. "We shall start again at first light."

Before Lukas could answer, the girl slipped away into the shadows. Only after a few moments did Lukas realize she had called him by his name.

For the next two days, they continued through the hills, now taking a turn to the north. The versifier's provisions had long since been shared out and the flask emptied. Had it been up to him, Lukas was sure they would have perished from hunger. At home, the only trees that interested him were those with ripe, stealable apples. None grew here. Nor could he tell one bush or plant from another. The versifier was equally at a loss. It was Nur-Jehan who dug in the ground for roots and plucked the sparse berries from unlikely-looking shrubs.

"With Saalab, we'd be feasting on shish kebab," moaned Kayim, "instead of these vile-tasting objects. Who'd ever dare to eat such fare? Make merry on a sour berry? And these mushrooms—you don't think she's trying to poison us?"

A sharper goad than hunger was thirst. Yet the girl seemed able to scent the smallest freshet. Once, as they trudged across a stretch of dry, yellowing shrub, Nur-Jehan halted an instant. Her nostrils flared; without a word, she loped ahead into a stand of trees.

By the time Lukas caught up with her, she had plunged into a rock-rimmed pool. Without hesitation, he dove after her. The shock of the icy water took his breath away. Moments before, he had been parched and roasting. Now his teeth chattered, he shivered wildly, and hurriedly splashed his way back to dry ground. The versifier was content merely to drink from his cupped hands and pour a little water on his sun-reddened scalp.

Nur-Jehan seemed in better spirits than Lukas had ever seen her. When she told them that it would be wiser to rest here and set out fresher at dawn, Lukas and Kayim eagerly agreed.

Nur-Jehan sat with arms clasped around her knees and gazed absently into the pool. While the versifier dipped his blistered toes, Lukas sprawled beside the girl.

"If you were home," he ventured, "what would you be doing now? Weaving? Sweeping? Tending goats?"

"They are honorable occupations." Then she added curiously, "What would you be doing in that town you spoke of?"

"Well, let me see. Maybe some service for the Mayor, just to keep him alert. Like the time I made him turn honest, though he never thanked me for it. That was when I taught a crow to say, 'Have a care, Your Honor. All is known!' I set it to roost on the Mayor's chimney one night. At the crack of dawn, the first thing the Mayor heard was a voice croaking down the flue, 'All is known! All is known!' He jumped out of bed, then and there went running as fast as he could to the Town Hall, and put back the bags of money he, ah, borrowed from the treasury. And he was still in his nightshirt—"

He stopped. The girl's shoulders were trembling and he wondered what he had said to make her weep. Then he saw that she had actually begun to giggle.

"King of Abadan, you are truly a rascal."

Lukas shrugged modestly. "I do the best I can."

Next day, as they drew closer to the massive stone lintels of the pass, Lukas realized the girl's goading and bullying had been deliberate. Without her, they would have been still blundering their way through the hills.

"Or giving the vultures an afternoon snack," agreed Kayim. "Yes, she's a good sort, once you get to know her," he admitted. "On the other hand, so is a wildcat— and I've never been eager to pursue that acquaintance."

Even so, Lukas felt that a knot had loosened, though not altogether come undone. The girl and the versifier continued to insult each other; but at least they grinned as they did so. If the girl seemed downcast or drawn into herself, Lukas's tales of his pranks at home never failed to make her laugh. For her part, she told him a little of the ways of Bishangar, of its mountains and crags she clearly loved.

"These are molehills against the heights of Bishangar," she said, gesturing around her. "The peak of Umm al-Raas—there, we are very close to the stars. Perhaps this is why we are different from the Abadanis."

"If indeed you are," said Lukas. "I doubt anyone can tell an Abadani star from a Bishangari star. Except, maybe, Locman."

Lukas also understood he could not push their friendship past a point as high and rocky as Umm al-Raas itself; and Nur-Jehan's anxiety to reach her own country grew sharper the closer they came to the valley of the Hazra.

"I told you once it was not important for you to know," the girl said, when he again ventured to ask why she was so anxious to get home. "I tell you now, for your own protection, it is not safe for you to know."

Her look convinced him it was useless to press further, and he said no more about it.

By noon, they reached the banks of the Hazra. Nearby stretched a wide and rutted pathway.

"Look there," said Kayim, pointing at the tracks in the dust. "This must have been the caravan. We've missed them again. They're ahead of us. With our luck, they could be most of the way to Turan."

Once more, they set off at a quick pace, this time the impatient versifier leading. After little more than an hour, Kayim shouted and clapped his hands:

"I see them! They've started pitching their tents. Come on, it's carpets and cushions for us! Sherbet and shish kebab! A few words with Saalab and we'll be treated royally—that is, in a manner of speaking."

CHAPTER
✷ 10 ✷

*T*he versifier, his mouth already watering, hurried along at a dogtrot, with Nur-Jehan and Lukas at his heels. Lukas, as they drew closer, could hear a babble of voices and he glimpsed a number of travelers sitting on the ground before their cook fires.

Kayim, who had outdistanced his companions, halted suddenly and turned back. His face was ashen. Nur-Jehan cried out and ran to him. Following her, Lukas now saw that what he had taken for cook fires were smoldering piles of baggage. Bales and bundles had been ripped open, their contents scattered over the plain. The pack camels had been stripped of their loads. Of horses, only a few swaybacked nags remained. The travelers huddled in the dust or wandered aimlessly through heaps of garments and goods.

There were many wounded, and these Nur-Jehan and Lukas tended as best they could. Kayim, having gone to look for the caravan leader, joined them a few moments later.

"Saalab is dead," he murmured. "A dozen others, too. It was Shir Khan and his band of robbers. Butchers! No one ever thought they'd come this far south; and that, no doubt, is exactly why they did. An hour sooner and we'd have been in the thick of it. For that matter, if we'd left with the caravan that morning—"

The more Kayim realized how narrow their escape had been, the more agitated he became, trembling, shaking his head, and muttering to himself. The survivors, numbering about a hundred, had meanwhile collected what goods they were able to carry, and in a ragged procession started on foot for Turan. The three fugitives plodded along with them for the sake of whatever concealment and safety the forlorn company provided. Nur-Jehan had salvaged a torn caftan and headcloth from the ruined baggage and could now pass easily for a young groom or camel driver.

"You, is it? Can't you outrun your bad luck?"

At this voice in his ear, Lukas turned to see Namash, the water seller. The stocky little man appeared unharmed and, despite his gruffness, genuinely pleased at finding Lukas.

"What was it last time we met? A bloody nose?" said Namash. "Now Shir Khan. Even so, what's to rob from you? You didn't have the price of a cup of water in Shirazan. How did you get the fee to travel in the caravan? I didn't see you when we started."

"As for money," Lukas broke in, "my two friends—"

"That pair of merchant princes? Don't tell me. You tagged along, and nobody the wiser. That's how you pulled it off. Never mind, I don't want to know. That's your business."

"And how's your own business?" put in Lukas, hoping to escape too close a questioning. "A water seller must do well on a caravan like this."

"What water seller?" Namash chuckled and grinned all over his face. "No more of that. I'll tell you something. It should cheer you up. Who knows, someday it could happen to you. I've come into a fortune. Like that! A snap of the fingers. Shir Khan never got a piece of it. Who thinks a poor water seller has a purse of gold in his water bag? Oh, they knocked me around for the sport of it, but that's as far as it went."

"Now you're a rich man," said Lukas, smiling to himself. "Aren't you afraid to tell me? I could be a robber myself."

Namash burst out laughing. "I know robbers! One kind or another, I've seen enough of them. You may be a step ahead of the constable; but a robber, no. Besides, I have to tell somebody. I still can't get over it. That day in the bazaar, you were my best customer, so you know how business was. By evening, I was ready to find a corner to sleep in. Then along comes an old fellow who says he's been looking for me. First he wants to cast my horoscope. As if I need to know my troubles ahead of time! Then he pulls out a purse, puts it in my hand, and that's the last I see of him."

Thanks to this miraculous windfall, Namash explained, he now meant to become a merchant, a dealer in foodstuffs of all kinds. Lukas wished him great prosperity, glad Locman had accomplished his errand. By this time, night had fallen and most of the ragtag caravan had stopped to rest. Nur-Jehan and Kayim squatted with Lukas beside the water seller.

"Here's one friend of King Kasha," said Lukas, with a nod in the direction of Namash.

"Is he, indeed?" said the versifier. "But wasn't there talk in Shirazan Bazaar? How the King pardoned a notorious rogue, some public versifier, and set him up like a prince when he should have stuck him up on a spear?"

"If he did," replied Namash, "he must have had a good reason for it."

"Oh, he did," said Kayim. "I know something of the case. The versifier was truly a delightful fellow and deserved every bit of good fortune. Believe me, I admire King Kasha as much as you do."

In addition to saving his purse, the former water seller had kept most of his provisions. These he shared with Lukas and his companions, urging them not to stint as he would soon buy fresh supplies for his journey northward.

Before they could take advantage of the generous offer, a wave of alarm spread among the travelers. A troop of horsemen, bearing torches, galloped into the makeshift camp. Dismounting, they went roughly among the terrified survivors, seizing first one, then another, and thrusting them aside. Lukas drew closer to Nur-Jehan. The officer striding through the encampment was Nahdir.

From what Lukas heard of the guards' questions, they were searching for two dangerous criminals and a Bishangari slave. Glancing around, Lukas wondered how they might take to their heels. The guards had posted themselves in a circle.

Namash suddenly jumped to his feet. "Three runaways?" he called, hurrying to Nahdir. "I can tell you where they are."

Stunned by this betrayal, Lukas braced himself for a hopeless struggle to escape. The water seller flung himself down before the Commander of Guards, and blurted, "I know where you can find them!"

Nahdir seized him by the jacket and shook him furiously. "Speak out, you worm!"

"Shir Khan! Shir Khan!" stammered the water seller. "He carried them off: two men and a Bishangari. The robbers took them. I saw it with my own eyes. They're long gone. That's the end of them, be sure of it. The Bishangari—they'll sell her over the east border. The other two, if they don't bring a good ransom—" Namash drew the edge of his hand across his throat. "That's the best they can hope for. That devil Shir Khan! In his hands, they're good as dead."

Adding to his account, the water seller pointed back toward Shirazan as the direction the bandits had taken with their captives. The Commander of Guards threw Namash aside. Without a word of thanks for the information, he turned on his heel and ordered his men to remount. As they galloped from the camp, Namash stumped back to Lukas and his companions.

"May I be forgiven for lying," said the water seller. "But, now I'm rich, I'll have to get used to doing it once in a while."

"Namash, we thank you," said Lukas. "You took a terrible risk. But why?"

"Say nothing, tell nothing, I want to know nothing," returned Namash. "Because there happens to be three of you, and one a Bishangari—Oh, I know Bishangaris like I know robbers—can I swear you're the ones they're after? You're a ragged lot, but if that's a crime we'd all go to jail. Besides, I think you brought me luck that day. So, let it go at that."

Namash, however, feared the Commander of Guards might return to question him further, and he thought it wise to leave the encampment immediately. Lukas thanked him again and wished him well. Nur-Jehan, too, would have gone without delay. This time, even the girl's authority could not budge the versifier now that the worst danger was over.

"Let come what may," declared Kayim, "I'm here to stay till break of day, then wend our way—no, not one more step do I move tonight."

Nur-Jehan finally agreed and they stretched themselves on the ground. By first light, nevertheless, the girl was already up and urging them to be moving again. Before the rest of the camp had begun to stir, the three set out for Turan. The city was not far and the girl judged that they could travel faster at this hour with less risk.

Before midday, they came in sight of drab stone walls baking in the harsh sun. At the outskirts of the city rose a few tents, and here and there a number of stalls and benches. Under a striped awning squatted a coarse-bearded man with a lopsided face. Alongside him were roped three horses. Lukas would have passed him by, but Nur-Jehan abruptly halted. Lukas followed her glance. She was staring at the tallest of the animals.

"That Abadani has taken Rakush."

"Are you sure?" began Lukas. "Those sorry nags—"

"Do I not know my own horse? The Abadani must have taken him on his way north, when I set him free. It could not have been easy. But it is Rakush. I will have him back."

"Yes, yes, of course you will," Lukas assured her, pulling the girl away from the horse trader's tent. "Give Kayim and me a chance to think—"

"What is to be thought?" the girl retorted. "I will have my horse or I will have the Abadani's life. The two of you go toward him, and I toward the horse line. Set upon him, while I—"

"Wait, wait!" cried Lukas. "That won't do."

The girl looked at him, puzzled.

"How so? You have your dagger, have you not? It will be enough."

"No daggers," Lukas protested. "None of that."

Nur-Jehan thought for a moment. "You are right. It will be best to attack him another way. Perhaps, if we set fire to his tent."

"No fires, either!" cried Lukas. "Are you out of your wits?"

"I do not understand." Nur-Jehan frowned. "How else will you set against him?"

"We don't," said Lukas. "We don't attack him at all."

"I will have Rakush."

"And so you will, I promise. Only cool down. If we go at it your way, we'll have the whole town about our ears. Then you'll never get your horse. What you'll get instead is killed."

Nur-Jehan stiffened. "Rakush would have given his life for me. I will do no less for him. I am not afraid to die."

"Well, I am," said Lukas, "especially when I don't have to. So leave off with attacks, fires, and whatever. We could trade the dagger for the horse. The blade must be worth more than the fellow sees in a year. But I don't like that idea. If he took the dagger in trade, then he'd have it and we wouldn't. No, the best thing is to get hold of Rakush with the horse trader none the wiser."

Nur-Jehan gave him a look of utmost horror. "Steal him? That is ignoble!"

"Yes, and practical, too," said Lukas. "For one thing, it isn't stealing. You're simply getting back your property in a quiet, friendly way."

"There is no honor in that."

"Not a bit," Lukas cheerfully agreed. "But there's a horse in it. Besides, if I have my way, we'll get Rakush as a gift and all of us come out alive. At the moment, staying alive should be honor enough."

CHAPTER

❧❧ *11* ❧❧

*W*arning Nur-Jehan and Kayim to keep out of sight, Lukas drew closer to the horse trader, whose name, he learned, was Katir. He glanced quickly at the white horse: hard-ridden, badly cared for. Its flanks were raw, its mouth cut; the mane hung tangled and dusty. Yet there was no mistaking the graceful head and proud bearing.

Lukas, however, paid no further attention to Rakush. He strode up to the first horse in the line, a rawboned, swaybacked mare. He patted the animal's neck and made a great show of pleasure and excitement.

Katir, squatting on a piece of carpet, was gnawing a chicken bone. At sight of Lukas, he jumped to his feet. The horse trader was thick-chested, with a red sash holding in his heavy belly. Lukas felt a momentary twinge. If his plan failed, he would have a large and furious bear of a man to deal with, and he thought unhappily of the fruit seller in Shirazan Bazaar.

"Beggar!" shouted Katir. "Keep away from those jades!"

"I won't harm them," said Lukas.

"No," returned the horse trader, "nor you won't be buying them, either."

"That's to be seen. I might buy one, or all, or none, depending on how they suit me. First, I'd like a word with them."

At that, Lukas made as if to whisper in the horse's ear; then put his own ear close to the animal's mouth. The horse whinnied. Lukas nodded eagerly:

"Yes, yes. Go on. Are you sure? Tell me again, to make certain."

"Here, what's all this?" demanded Katir, tossing aside his chicken bone. He seized Lukas by the collar. "Talking to a horse? You're a half-wit! Be gone, or I'll knock the other half out of your head."

"O Generous Prince of Horse Traders," replied Lukas, "I thank you. Your fine mare has told me all I need to know."

"Eh?" grunted Katir. "May I have the seven-year itch and only two years to scratch if that nag can say one word."

"You can't speak her language?" said Lukas. "What a pity, Most Unfortunate of Equine Purveyors, for you'd be rich. As rich as I'll soon be."

Katir squinted at Lukas. "There's money in this? Let my beard fall out if I don't take my share."

"Treasure by the bushel. That's what your mare tells me. These creatures know many secrets. It's only a matter of asking and understanding what they say. If you doubt me, I'll prove it. Stay here, I'll be back in no time."

Slipping from the grasp of the bewildered Katir, Lukas trotted around the angle of the city wall. There, well out of sight, he leaned against the stones, and whistled to pass the time. When he judged the horse trader had waited long enough, he ran back, pushed past Katir, and dropped to his knees in front of the mare:

"Blessings on you, Wisest of Animals! May you enjoy the bottomless feed bag of my gratitude!"

"Leave off!" ordered Katir, hauling Lukas to his feet. "Next you'll tell me you've made a fortune this past half hour."

"Indeed I have. Here, what better proof?"

So saying, Lukas reached under his shirt and pulled out the Royal Dagger. Seeing the costly blade, Katir's eyes began glittering more than the gem-studded weapon. Lukas went on:

"Your mare told me to go a quarter league east of the wall, then eight paces left, and look under the second white stone. I did as she said, and this is what I found. My thanks again for the use of her. Now I'll be on my way."

"No you won't," cried the horse trader, clutching

Lukas with one heavy hand and holding out the other. "Let's have that knife. It was my horse told you where to find it, so it belongs to me."

Lukas shrugged. "If you want this trifle so badly, you're welcome to it." He tossed Katir the dagger. "Here, take it. We'll part friends. Too bad you'll lose so much for the sake of such a trinket.

"Oh, yes, she says there's more to be found, and those two friends of hers know even greater treasures. But, as you say, they're your horses. Talk to them yourself. Mind you, though, be courteous with them or they'll tell you nothing."

"May nettles grow from your nose!" burst out Katir. "You know I can't understand a word they say!"

"You'll get the knack of it," Lukas assured him. "Learning their language, the grammar and all that, should be no trouble at all for a quick-witted fellow like you. But I admit there's one small difficulty: their accents. Now, your northern horse has one way of talking; your southern, another. And your strawberry roan, different from either. Be wary of that. Misunderstand and you're likely to get the directions wrong and go straggling all over the country. Aside from that, there's nothing to it. I can teach you. It would only take eight or nine years."

"That won't answer!" cried the horse trader. "I can't keep letters in my head long enough to write my name. And you'd have me cram in all those horse languages!"

"A pity," sighed Lukas. "You might as well be dragging a treasure chest and never have the key to open it. I'm sorry for you."

As Lukas turned on his heel, Katir shouted after him, "Wait! We're not done yet."

"Aren't we?" said Lukas. "You have a fine dagger to sell. Whatever you get would be a piddling price when you think what you might have gained. Even so, be satisfied."

"Satisfied with this—this nothing? When I can have a hundredfold its worth? Do you take me for a fool? Here, listen to what I'll do for you." The horse trader's eyes grew beady as he lowered his voice.

"You understand these beasts, eh? Now, you travel along with me and tell me what they say, where to find gold and all such. I'm an honest man, you can see that. Openhanded, too generous for my own good. So, whatever these bone-bags let us find, you'll have your share, a fat one. Take my word on that."

Lukas shook his head. "Why share at all? These aren't the only horses in Abadan. No, thank you just the same, I'll have a few words with the next one I meet. Farewell."

"Hold on," said Katir. "For all you know, it could be some stupid beast, or some pauper nag without a copper to its name."

"That's the risk," admitted Lukas. "But once you lay hands on all those riches, how can I be sure you won't cheat me? After all, you made me give you the dagger."

"Take it back!" bellowed the horse trader. "Here, it's yours."

"Oh, I couldn't do that," said Lukas. "You have the right to your own goods. So, I'll be on my way."

Seeing his riches melt away before he could lay a finger on them, Katir pulled off his headcloth, threw it down, and stamped on it:

"My last offer! Keep the dagger! Only jabber a little with those nags and tell me where I'll find more."

"A hard bargain," said Lukas, reluctantly allowing Katir to press the Royal Dagger into his hand. "But, O Golden Tongued, who can resist your eloquence?"

Still ignoring Rakush, Lukas went to the second horse, whispered in its ear, and made a show of listening attentively:

"How's that again? Five leagues north? Turn right and go a hundred paces? A tree with a circle carved on it. Dig under the roots. Yes, yes, I understand. A chest with bars of gold. Sacks of diamonds. What, no emeralds? Ah, well, that will have to do."

Turning to Katir, he repeated the instructions. The horse trader, gnawing his thumbs impatiently, would have set off then and there. Lukas halted him:

"Let's hear what this last one tells us," he said, pointing at Rakush. He whispered in the stallion's ear and, as before, pretended to listen.

"Oho, the best yet," Lukas declared after ending his earnest conversation with Rakush. "This horse knows more than the other two. And so he should. He tells me he was the King's favorite, with his own stable in Shirazan Palace. He ate his oats from a golden bucket, wore trappings of silk. He also tells me," added Lukas, "that you stole him."

"He's a liar!" exclaimed Katir.

"I'm only repeating what he says. You broke into the Royal Stables, crept into his stall—"

"No! I found him running wild in the hills. The others—ah, well, I might have taken them a little before their masters were ready to part with them. But not this one. I tell you I found him."

"Not according to him."

"Who are you going to believe?" cried Katir. "An honest man or some vagabond horse?" He strode up to Rakush and shook his fist. "Tell the truth, you lying beast!"

"Who cares?" said Lukas. "The main thing is he knows a treasure trove. A cave filled with riches—"

"Don't listen to a word of it," retorted Katir. "He lied about the rest, and he's lying now. He'd lead me on some wild-goose chase. Faithless brute! You can't trust anyone these days."

"I'm afraid you're right," said Lukas. "Better pay him no mind. He's likely to tell you all manner of nonsense. There's nothing worse than a lying horse. Incurable."

"To the devil with him!" cried the horse trader. "I won't waste feed on the truthless beast. Take him, he's yours. And out of my way!"

Not troubling to fold his tent or roll up his carpet, the horse trader leaped astride the mare. With the second horse trailing after him, Katir set off to the north as fast as the swaybacked steed would carry him, and soon was lost to sight in a cloud of dust.

Lukas whistled for Nur-Jehan and Kayim. Seeing his mistress, Rakush whinnied joyfully as the girl flung her arms about his neck.

The versifier wagged his head in admiration as Lukas told how he had dealt with Katir.

"As a king," said Kayim, "you made some blunders. As a fig stealer, disastrous. For swindling a horse trader, I have to say you're matchless. What's wrong? You should be crowing."

"No," said Lukas, "I spoiled it. How could I have been such a fool? What a bargain I missed!"

"What are you grumbling about?" asked Kayim. "You got Rakush as a gift. You kept the dagger. You sent Katir on such a fool's errand we'll never see him again."

"True," said Lukas. "But I should have made him throw in a saddle."

Nur-Jehan turned to him and reluctantly said, "You did better than I would have done. I am grateful. I have Rakush unharmed, and the Abadani suffers no more than a fruitless ride to satisfy his greed. It was not noble, but perhaps there are times when it is nobler to be prudent."

"At last! Now you're showing good sense!" cried Lukas. The girl was looking at him with considerably more respect than she had ever shown and he could not help feeling a little puffed up. He smiled at her indulgently. "I hope you've learned something.

"Look after Rakush," he went on. "Kayim and I will find out if there's any news in the bazaar." He handed her the dagger. "Keep this. I doubt you'll need it, but just in case. And besides, I'd rather not take it with me. There're too many light-fingered rascals abroad."

While Nur-Jehan set about rubbing down the white stallion and untangling his mane, Lukas and the versifier hurried into Turan Bazaar. The city, smaller and dustier than Shirazan, boasted no spires and domes, only a jumble of low-roofed buildings pressing one against the other. The bazaar, too, was smaller but no less boisterous. Kayim, with his knack for scraping acquaintances among peddlers and cameleers, quickly learned that no rumors of any kind had yet spread from Shirazan Palace.

Relieved, the two went back to Katir's abandoned tent, anxious to make new plans. Lukas glanced around. There was no sign of the girl. The horse was gone.

"What's happened? Nahdir's men? No, that couldn't be." He ran from one stall to the other, calling the girl's name. In growing alarm, he started through the city gate, thinking she might have followed into the bazaar. Kayim was shouting for him. He raced to the side of the versifier.

"Save your steps." Kayim grimaced. "The pot seller over there says he saw a young whelp in a dirty caftan gallop off on a horse as if the devil himself were after them. They're long gone: girl, horse, dagger, and all. If you ask me, I'd say it's for the best. But you taught her a good lesson. Oh, that you did! She's a fast learner."

"Damned wretch!" Lukas burst out. "Treacherous little brigand! Miserable, scheming, conniving goat-girl!"

"That," said Kayim, "sounds like you've gone and fallen in love with her."

"Worse," Lukas answered bitterly. "I liked her."

CHAPTER

❈❈ *12* ❈❈

Cheer up," said the versifier. "When sweet friends part, a broken heart is sure to smart. There's only one remedy. Find some new sort of mischief. Your Bishangari stole the dagger, which we could have sold for a pretty price. There's a distinct aroma of stable about Katir's trappings, but at least we have something over our heads. That leaves only the small matter of keeping body and soul together. We can't risk running afoul of the law. So, much as I hate to admit it, we may have to consider a very painful prospect, honest work."

Kayim sighed. "I see no way out of it. Well, you showed me a good trick. Let me show you a thing or two. Turan isn't the liveliest spot in the world. But my talent will shine all the brighter without a shabby lot of second-rate competitors to cast their shadows on it."

The versifier strode jauntily through the Turan gate.

Lukas trudged after him, chin on chest, still unable to grasp that Nur-Jehan had so betrayed his friendship. The noisy bazaar did nothing to lift his spirits. Despite his angry, bitter thoughts, his curiosity roused when Kayim, finding space in the middle of the square, clapped his hands sharply and whistled through his teeth.

Having thus caught the attention of a few idlers, the versifier began waving his arms and, like a camel driver, shouting orders as loudly and convincingly as if the animal were at his side.

These antics drew more passersby. The versifier kept on with his commands, grumbling that his beast was lazy and ill-tempered. At last, one of the onlookers remarked that this fellow was either out of his wits or his camel had wandered off and he was too foolish to have noticed it.

"You can't see my camel?" returned Kayim, after ordering the invisible animal to kneel and behave himself. "Too bad, friend, because he's extremely valuable: the same breed as the camel of Hakim Luti."

Judging that enough onlookers had gathered to make it worth his while, Kayim squatted on the ground and beckoned his listeners to do likewise.

"There was a famous rogue named Hakim Luti," Kayim began. "One day in the bazaar, he stopped at a fruit seller's booth. All of a sudden, Hakim started shouting, beating the air with a stick, and crying:

" 'Greedy beast! Do I have to keep an eye on you

every moment? Stop, you wretch! May you grow seven humps and have the rheumatism in every one!'

"Hakim then begged the merchant's forgiveness for the camel's gobbling so much fruit. 'Just look at the thieving brute,' said Hakim. 'Swallowing those beautiful grapes! As if he hadn't already made away with a dozen of your best apricots.'"

"Hold on there," put in one of the onlookers. "You're not going to tell us the fruit seller believed anything like that. How could he see a camel when there wasn't one to be seen?"

"Of course he didn't see the camel," agreed the versifier. "But then Hakim stepped up to him, all humble apologies, and offered to pay for whatever damage his animal had done.

"'That's only fair,' said Hakim. 'After all, he's been munching away at those piles of fruit for who knows how long. If I hadn't caught him when I did, he might have eaten your whole stock in trade. Well, you know your wares better than I do, so count up what he's eaten and tell me what it comes to. I'll give you whatever price you ask, and it's a good lesson for me to keep a better watch on him.'

"The merchant saw neither hide nor hair of Hakim's camel. But, here was a fellow offering to pay for what the beast had eaten, and the merchant wasn't going to be such a fool as to say no. In fact, the more he thought of it the better bargain it was. So he answered:

" 'Well, there's the grapes first of all. Apricots, too— you saw them with your own eyes. But here, wait a minute, I'm looking over my goods and I see straight off that camel of yours ate up a bushel of my dates.'

" 'As much as that?' said Hakim. 'Well, add it to the reckoning.'

" 'Then I have to count six ripe melons,' the peddler went on.

" 'Six melons! The brute must have swallowed them whole! What an appetite he has!'

" 'So he does,' agreed the peddler. 'But those invisible camels, they're the worst kind. Greedy devils, they'd stuff themselves morning to night if you'd let them. They can't help it. That's their nature. Take my advice and sell him quick as you can. Because now I see he's eaten most of a dozen oranges.'

" 'Oranges, too?' wailed Hakim. 'He's going to burst! No matter, reckon them up with everything else.'

" 'And five pomegranates,' went on the peddler. 'But I'll be honest and tell you they were a little shriveled, so I'll throw them in for nothing.'

"The peddler then made a show of counting on his fingers and told Hakim how much it all came to.

" 'That's high,' said Hakim, 'but if that's what you say my camel has eaten, I won't question it.'

"Hakim made as if to reach into his purse. Before he took out any money, he suddenly let out a yell and began hopping on one leg, howling in pain.

"The peddler stared at him. 'Now, friend, what's happened to you?'

" 'You ask me that?' cried Hakim. 'You saw for yourself this very moment. That dog of yours! Vicious cur! He's taken a bite out of my leg!'

" 'Away with you!' cried the peddler. 'There's no dog here!'

" 'Don't try to make a fool of me,' answered Hakim, between groans. 'I know when I've been bitten. How dare you keep a dangerous dog like that! He's a threat to life and limb.'

" 'No dog,' flung back the peddler. 'Where is he, then? You show him to me.'

" 'He's right there, the ill-tempered beast,' replied Hakim, 'sitting beside my camel. Well, that's not the end of it, my fine fellow. Your dog bit me and I claim damages.' And Hakim named a sum twice what the peddler had demanded. 'But I'll be as fair with you as you were with me. Take off what you were going to charge me for the fruit. Now, for the rest, let's have it, cash in hand.'

" 'Not a penny,' declared the peddler. 'Do you think I'll pay you for a bite from an invisible dog? Go whistle for it!'

" 'But,' said Hakim, 'you didn't stint when it came to charging me for invisible fruit that my invisible camel ate. So, my greedy friend, you'd better settle with me or we'll both go before the magistrate. And how would your tale sound then?'

"Grumbling and cursing all such rogues, the peddler paid out the money. And Hakim Luti went off, leading his invisible camel."

His tale ended, Kayim grinned around him expectantly. Lukas made ready to pick up whatever coins would be thrown.

Instead of money, the listeners showered the versifier with groans:

"What kind of foolishness is that?" one declared. "How could this Hakim see a dog that wasn't there? Suppose the peddler hadn't paid, and they went to the magistrate? They'd have been laughed out of court. And how much did the peddler ask in the first place?"

"That's right," added another. "We should know that, what with the price of grapes, oranges, and all."

"What's that peddler's name?" put in a third. "He doesn't trade in Turan Bazaar. As for Hakim Luti, I never heard of him."

The crowd drifted away. Too crestfallen to attempt rekindling their interest, the versifier told Lukas he was through for the day.

"Nit-pickers," muttered Kayim. "They don't appreciate the finer points of style."

With empty pockets and emptier bellies, Lukas and the versifier trudged back to the horse trader's tent.

The following morning, they returned to the bazaar. In addition to his tale-telling, Kayim juggled with half-a-dozen tent pegs. Lukas, taking his own turn, spun cartwheels and somersaults, danced on his hands, and whistled through his teeth at the same time. A few coins were thrown; but the next day, fewer.

"I think, my friend, we'd better move on," Kayim glumly told Lukas. "In Shirazan, Hakim Luti and his invisible camel always did well for me. So did the juggling. In Turan, I fear, good taste is a waste, and sadly misplaced."

Packing up the horse trader's abandoned gear and shouldering the bundles, they set out for the nearest city, Hamaveran. There, Lukas ventured to tell some of the tales that once had made Nur-Jehan laugh; but they met with little more success than Hakim Luti and the camel. For the next several weeks, they pressed on, making their way from one town to the other, hoping to mend their fortunes. In one village, they traded their tales and juggling for sheepskin jackets and two pairs of boots; in another, they were lucky to scrape a meager dinner.

The versifier had given up shaving his head and the vanity of curling his moustache, which had regrown to impressive length. It sprawled under his nose, spread across his face, and nearly lost itself in a thicket of tangled hair.

If the versifier hardly resembled his former self, Lukas was equally changed. Afraid to use his own name, he now called himself "al-Ukash." Uncomfortable at first, he grew accustomed to it, and to his own appearance. The skin of his cheeks and brow had blistered, shredded away, and come back tougher, to be further coarsened by dust and grit. His eyes were red-rimmed from the wind, his face more sun-blackened than Nur-Jehan's. He doubted the girl would recognize him.

In the bazaar at Khana-Kazra, they heard the news: King Kasha was dead; Shugdad had proclaimed himself ruler of Abadan.

"He was bound to do it." Lukas gave a dry laugh. "Dead—it gives me an odd feeling. Does he really believe it? I hope so. At least he won't be looking for us. Or is it deliberate eyewash? In any case, for a dead man I maintain a remarkable appetite."

To his satisfaction, the townsfolk greeted the news without celebration. An air of bitterness sharpened at a further decree. All able-bodied men were commanded to join the Royal Armies. Those who disobeyed would be taken up by the King's Officers and sent in fetters to penal companies.

"You'd better come down with a limp," muttered Kayim. "And the limper the better."

"Easily done," said Lukas. "I'm footsore already. What's your ailment to be?"

"How's that again?" The versifier cupped an ear. "I can't hear a word you say."

With the King's Officers abroad, Lukas and the versifier dared stay no longer than a day in each town. They had, this while, been drifting generally westward. Kayim now suggested veering north along the Harami foothills, where the outlying towns might be too isolated to draw the Officers' scrutiny.

"Wherever you want," Lukas wearily agreed. "One place or another, it makes no difference. Stay, move on, it's pointless either way."

"That never troubled you in Zara-Petra, from what you've told me."

"It's different, somehow," said Lukas. "I was an idler because I wanted to be one, not because I had to. I cared for nothing; now I have nothing to care for."

By week's end they came to Bayaz, more village than city, drowsing in the shelter of a narrow valley. The white, flat-roofed buildings stood unwalled, and they entered without being questioned or challenged. Here, unlike some of the other towns, they saw no sign of troops assembling. Though it appeared safe to halt, the versifier doubted his talents would stir any interest in the sleepy little bazaar. To their surprise, they were eagerly welcomed. The townsfolk roared with laughter even at the tale of Hakim Luti's camel. Lukas had embroidered his account of the Mayor and the talking crow. The delighted listeners demanded to hear more.

The versifier had just finished a turn at juggling when a neatly garbed manservant approached, bowed respectfully, and declared that the Mayor of Bayaz desired to be entertained by the travelers.

"Marvelous!" chuckled Kayim. "They may be off the beaten track, but I give them credit for good taste."

The servant led them through a courtyard and pleasant garden, conducted them to an airy, well-swept chamber, sparsely furnished with only a few cushions heaped against the white plaster wall.

"I've heard of rich men filling a versifier's mouth with gold," whispered Kayim. "That's hardly to be expected here. But if they fill up our mouths with stewed chicken or a bit of mutton, that will suit me as well."

The versifier broke off his speculation. A gaunt, white-robed figure had stepped through the doorway. Lukas stared and his jaw dropped. It was Locman.

Calling his name, Lukas ran toward the Astrologer, who peered and blinked for several moments before recognizing his visitors.

"Locman, whatever brought you here? I'm happy to see you safe and sound. Are you the Mayor's Astrologer?"

"Astrologer, not exactly," answered Locman. "As for the Mayor, I have the honor of occupying that office myself. When I was told two strangers had come to Bayaz, never did I suspect—Ah, forgive me, Center of the Universe, the surprise has made me quite forget proper courtesy."

With that, the Astrologer creaked down on his knees and, with some difficulty, touched his brow to the floor.

"No need for that," said Lukas, helping Locman to

his feet. "I'm not King of Abadan. It's Shugdad now. You haven't heard the news."

"On the contrary," said Locman. "Word reaches us in Bayaz, though not as quickly as elsewhere, and we feel free to ignore it. Yes, I know of the Grand Vizier's proclamation. But I hasten to give you absolute assurance. You are still the rightful King of Abadan."

*A*las, my books, as well as all my charts and compendium of observations, were left behind in Shirazan Palace. Otherwise, you would see the law with your own eyes. The Vizier's claim is meaningless. There can be no new King unless the old one is guilty of some heinous treachery; or in fact is dead; or the end of his reign confirmed by the most reliable prophecy. Since none of those conditions apply, King you are and King you remain."

"No thanks to Shugdad," put in Lukas. "Especially the condition of being dead. You surely know what happened that night, the same night I asked you to go on an errand for me, if you remember."

"Indeed I do," answered Locman. "As you commanded, I gave a purse of money to a water seller. When I returned to Shirazan Palace, I found the Grand Vizier —I should not be overstating the case were I to say, noticeably upset. An attempt had been made on the King's life, the most embarrassing aspect being that it did not succeed. I considered the Vizier's conduct abominable, unforgivable, and I told him so."

"You dared take my side? At least I had one friend in the palace."

"Yes, in a personal sense," replied Locman. "But the truly disgraceful part was that none of it had been predicted. In all my observations there was not the slightest clue that you were to be assassinated. The Vizier should have had the decency to consult me. I could have assured him his plot was doomed to fail.

"True, Shugdad tried to set matters right, shall we say, in retrospect. He commanded me to prophesy, by the strongest signs and portents, that he was to be King of Abadan."

"I don't see why he bothered," said Lukas. "He was ready to have me strangled. What difference would a prophecy make?"

"A villain is always happier with some justification for his villainy," replied the Astrologer. "Indeed, the deeper the villainy the loftier the pretext. But, naturally, I refused to give a false prophecy. The stars, as it seemed to me, were not to be tampered with. Shugdad threatened to have me impaled, flayed alive—the Vizier has no respect for personal dignity. So, I fled for my life, leaving all my possessions behind me. As Court Astrologer, I concerned myself with the grand spheres of policy and high matters of state. After my departure, I chose to narrow this view and offer my services in a more individual fashion."

"What I think he means," Kayim whispered to Lukas, "is that he took up fortune-telling. Well, it's a living, and no more disreputable than versifying."

The light had faded. Servants came with lamps and trays of food. Lukas and the versifier ate eagerly, but the Astrologer scarcely picked at the dishes before him. Locman's robe of white wool, his fleecy cap, and his other garments were fresh and new; but Lukas noticed the Astrologer's eyes were somber. The furrows in his brow and cheeks had deepened, and there remained none of the almost childlike delight he had once shown. This troubled Lukas, and he said, "Since then, you must have done well for yourself. No offense, Locman, but you look —well, different. Though I suppose I do, too."

"I did well," answered Locman. "Or so I thought. In time, I made my way to Jabarsa, a pleasant little village where they received me cordially, feasted me, and showed me every favor. I had been there only three days when Shir Khan and his band fell upon us. They found no booty worth the taking, and so contented themselves with burning and killing. All were put to the sword. I was wounded and left for dead.

"My injury was not grievous, and I was able to tend it myself. For the villagers, alas, I could do nothing. I sat amid the ashes and pondered why others perished while I was spared. Of the many reasons I expounded, as I closely examined them none signified better than another. I reproached myself for not having predicted such a disaster and thereby saving those unfortunates. But there had been no sign, no warning in any of my calculations. I excused myself this failing, since my books and charts had been left in Shirazan. As I had no heart to remain, nor any great will to leave the ruins, I took a stick and set about scratching new computations in the dust, endeavoring to determine what path I should now follow.

"To these diagrams I devoted all my science, and toiled over them for several days. But, scarcely had I completed them when suddenly a wind rose from the hills, and blew across the village with such force that in a single instant all my labor was scattered.

"I could have wept at the loss. The excellence of my science, as I then believed, lay in its order and symmetry, in the proper balancing of calculation, as fixed as the circuits of the stars. And yet, without sense or reason, the folk of Jabarsa had been slain and I still lived. Likewise, my days of careful computation had been set at nought by a gust of wind.

"I wondered, then, if indeed the world wagged as much by accident, past all calculations of my astrology. Taking what comfort I could from this, I set off in no direction at all; that is, taking whatever random path suited my fancy.

"I soon arrived in Bayaz, where I determined to set myself up once again as a prophet and soothsayer. Until then, I had taken great pains in the casting of horoscopes, in the refinement of my predictions. Now I followed a different procedure.

"Obtaining a number of scraps of paper, on them I inscribed whatever notions popped into my head at the moment; inscriptions of deepest wisdom I mixed with the most arrant nonsense, and shuffled and tossed them until I had no idea of their order or content. Even to me they were entirely incomprehensible. Their meanings, if indeed they held any, were susceptible to every manner of interpretation.

"My first client was a prosperous dealer in copperware, who desired to consult me on what course to follow in a certain affair of business. After hearing his question, I threw my papers on the ground, chose the first slip that came to hand, and presented it to the merchant. He studied it closely, then cried, 'Marvel of marvels! Here it is clearly set down! Exactly what I had in mind to do!'

"Paying me a generous fee, the merchant departed in great excitement. Next day, however, he returned downcast, moaning and beating his breast at losing most of his fortune.

"At first, I expected him to upbraid me or, depending on his disposition, break my head; and I made ready to defend myself against either eventuality. But he only wailed, 'O Wisest of Soothsayers! O Wonder of Ineffable Knowledge! Had I studied your advice more carefully and understood it better, I would have been the richest man in Bayaz. O Light in Darkness! I beseech you! Instruct me in what I now should do.'

"At random, I chose another paper. The merchant read it, nodding his head and showing every sign of satisfaction:

" 'Remarkable! Incredible! This reveals precisely what I suspected all along!'

"He hurried off, but soon returned and, to my astonishment, showered me with gold pieces. He had not only regained his fortune, but trebled it.

"I concluded, then, that in fact the world goes its way without regard whatever for predictions, sensible or otherwise. There is, alas, no plan or pattern we can follow with absolute assurance. The only certainty is uncertainty. The more calculation, the greater likelihood of all being set topsy-turvy: by a whim, a trifle, an inconsequential detail.

"And so I continued with my slips of paper. Soon I had more trade than I could manage: men and women of all ages and conditions, merchants, speculators, lovers, jealous wives and suspicious husbands, doctors of law and medicine. Though most of them followed their own inclinations and did what they intended in the first place, I gained fame and fortune. My wisdom and judgment were so praised that I was acclaimed Mayor of Bayaz. The townsfolk are overjoyed with me; and I assure you, Center of the Universe, if I have done no better than my predecessors in office, I have done no worse."

Locman's servants then led Lukas and Kayim to a chamber where couches had been arranged. The versifier immediately flung himself onto the cushions. Lukas, despite his fatigue, paced restlessly.

"Kayim," he said at last, "I've been thinking of this ever since Locman told me. Do you realize—I'm still King of Abadan!"

"Of course you are," the versifier sleepily answered, "in a fine point of law. If it makes you feel better, I'll gladly call you Center of the Universe or Kasha the Magnificent or anything that suits your fancy. What's the use of it? You might as well name yourself King of the Camels for all the good it will do you."

"Will you be my Grand Vizier?"

"Naturally," yawned Kayim. "Then we'll both have splendid titles that mean nothing to anyone."

"They will," said Lukas. "To another king. To Ardashir. I'm going to Bishangar."

CHAPTER

❈❈ *14* ❈❈

*T*his brought the versifier bolt upright and wide awake. "To Bishangar? You've lost your mind! There's no harm thinking yourself a king. But when you start acting like one, that's trouble."

"Nur-Jehan once told me that Ardashir wants peace. So do most of the Abadanis, from all I've seen and heard. They'll hold with me, not Shugdad. If I can talk with Ardashir face to face, we can try to settle without bloodshed."

"That's what you think," replied the versifier. "That brigand will snap you up like a crocodile, if you're unlucky enough to find him in the first place."

"I'll have to risk it. If Shugdad has his way, what kind of life will that be for any of us? I used to think Battisto would bring me home, one moment or the next. But who can guess what goes on in his head? Whether he cares what happens, or whether it's no more than a joke to him."

"If it is," said Kayim, "I don't appreciate his sense of humor."

"He may not be in Zara-Petra any more, for all I know," Lukas went on. "He could have had an accident. He could even be dead. There's no sense in what he did to me. A whim, a fancy, as Locman says. And for me, hunted from one place to another, that's no kind of life, either. If it's all Battisto's joke, if there's no sense in any of this, then I'll have to make my own sense of it."

"The joke, my friend, may turn out to be on you."

"I can't order you to go with me," said Lukas. "It might even be wiser if you stayed in Bayaz."

"Much wiser," agreed Kayim. "But, a king without his grand vizier?" The versifier sighed. "I've come this far, I might as well go the rest of the way. Grand vizier is a few steps down from being a versifier. Even so, Kayim, Grand Vizier of Abadan—it does have a certain ring to it."

On that, the versifier pulled the covers over his head and went back to snoring. Lukas was too restless to do more than drowse. In the morning, he was eager to tell Locman of his plan.

"I shall gladly draw out one of my papers for you," said the Astrologer. "Though I did not serve you well in the past, King of Abadan, perhaps I may now serve you better."

"Don't blame yourself," said Lukas. "You did all you

could, considering what you knew of me. You see, in the palace, I didn't tell you the whole truth."

"What king does?" put in Kayim. "A wise policy, as truth only tends to confuse matters. That's why I prefer versifying."

"My unfortunate King," said Locman, after Lukas explained how he had come to Shirazan and what he now intended, "you are neither quite one thing nor another, neither fully here nor there. As for your plan, yes, Shugdad has declared himself King, but he is shrewd enough to sense that the people of Abadan do not favor him. He requires a triumph, a great victory that will set the seal on his kingship. If he is denied that victory, if he fails to conquer Bishangar, I agree: His subjects will turn against him."

"Then my plan is sound," said Lukas.

"Alas, no plan is sound," corrected the Astrologer, "as I have already shown you."

"He wasn't paying attention," said Kayim. "That's another kingly habit."

"Seeking Ardashir is one thing," continued Locman. "Finding him, another. The King of the Bishangaris is a great fox. He changes ground swiftly, he goes to earth in one place and springs forth in another. This is one of his strengths. Shugdad will try to force him into a pitched battle, and crush him by weight of numbers. But, if Shugdad will have difficulty finding him, how much more difficult will it be for you."

"I won't find him," said Lukas. "I'll let him find me."

The versifier shook his head. "You have your work cut out for you. I only hope your work doesn't cut you out, if you take my meaning."

They stayed another day in Bayaz while Locman, at his own cost, secured two sturdy ponies, furnishings, and provisions. For weapons, however, Lukas accepted only a short knife. Taking leave of the Astrologer, they continued northward. Three days of hard travel brought them to the foothills near the Bishangari border. On the fourth morning, as they approached a clearing, Lukas suddenly reined up. So far, they had met no other travelers. Now, just ahead, several roughly garbed men squatted around the embers of a cook fire. Horses, tethered at the fringe of trees, kicked at their heel ropes.

"Royal Officers, do you think?" Lukas said under his breath.

"Not that crew," muttered Kayim. "If anything, they're on the run from Shugdad's army. Whoever they are, I'd rather not stop and chat."

"Neither would I. Pass around them."

The men, however, had already sighted the pair. Hailing them, two of the band ran to catch hold of the ponies' bridles and led them into the clearing, where their fellows beckoned them toward the pot of stewing meat. It was too late for Lukas to do anything but dismount. He gestured for Kayim to do the same, though not at all reassured by the way his hosts had begun examining the ponies and fingering the baggage. Meantime, a thickset man with a sheepskin cap on the back of his head had come out of the tent.

The others drew aside and one called out, "Ho, Lion of the World! Your guests await your welcome."

"I am called al-Ukash," began Lukas, as the man strode up to him. "My companion is Kayim."

"A public versifier," Kayim hastily put in. "Very friendly. Absolutely harmless."

"You shall recite for us all you know." The man stank of burned meat and old blood. A scruff of beard covered his pitted face. He narrowed his eyes at Lukas. "And you, al-Ukash? Are you friendly? I think not. You would have gone by us without so much as a greeting. That is not the way of a friend."

"There are King's Officers abroad, searching out men for the army. We thought you might be of them." Lukas grinned at him. "We aren't eager to be soldiers."

"Nor we, al-Ukash. Ah, such times we live in. We are humble traders, poor merchant travelers, making what bargains come to hand. You have goods? Show them. We will give you a generous price."

"That's the first piece of good luck we've had," replied Lukas, putting on the best face he could, though he had gone suddenly cold to the marrow of his bones. He was about to be robbed, of that he was certain; unarmed, not daring to fight free of these brigands, his only hope was to be robbed of as little as possible.

The self-styled merchant trader, meantime, had been smiling and bobbing his head, clasping his hands in a fawning gesture. Suddenly the man's boot shot out and drove sharply against Lukas's ankle. Caught unaware by the attack, and gasping with the pain of it, he lost his balance and tumbled to the ground. With an angry cry, the versifier started forward. Lukas gave him a warning glance. "Fight and we're dead," he muttered between clenched teeth.

"King's Officer? Stinking merchant?" The man laughed down at him. "I am Shir Khan! The Lion of the World!"

"So you are called." Lukas struggled to his feet and tried to hold himself upright. "Yes, a mighty lion. How is it, then, the lion preys on sheep? That is work for jackals. I have heard of your glorious victory at Jabarsa. Boldly done, O Lion! Mud huts and a few graybeards! And was there not a caravan attacked outside Turan? Travelers unarmed, trembling in their boots! I think, Shir Khan, this lion may be no more than a tame cat."

Shir Khan struck him across the face. "You are a dead man, al-Ukash, even as you stand. Before Turan, there were a dozen fought against us. It was I who cut down three with my own hands—"

Lukas never took his eyes from Shir Khan, who was so goaded that he seemed about to foam at the mouth in his rage.

"Forgive me for doubting your bravery," Lukas said quickly. "The prize was surely worth the bloodshed. As I've heard it told from one who was on that caravan, it was big as a pigeon's egg. What a ruby it must have been! What a price it must have brought!"

"Ruby?" burst out Shir Khan. "I sold no ruby."

"You kept it? You still have it?" Lukas shook his head. "A gem that size? It is good that you trust your men, Shir Khan. Even the most honest would be tempted by such a stone."

"There was none! This is bazaar gossip!"

Shir Khan's henchmen, during this, had come to stand closer to their chief. Lukas's talk of a ruby had set them to muttering among themselves. One, rawboned and swarthy, with two daggers in his sash, finally raised his voice:

"Lion of the World, how is it that nothing was said of this ruby until now?"

Shir Khan spun around. "You dare to question me like some bazaar pickpocket? I tell you there was no gem taken from the caravan. Have a care, Mansouri, I've heard your grumbling before, when spoils were divided."

"When ill-divided," returned Mansouri. "This is not the first time, Shir Khan, and I am not the only one to question how goods were shared."

"Do you say I cheated you?" cried Shir Khan. "Come out with it, then, to my face."

"I should not have spoken of this," put in Lukas. "Idle tongues make tales out of nothing. Gossip, nothing more. If the Lion of the World says he did not hold back a ruby, who doubts his word? No matter that Nahdir

Aga himself was hunting for you outside Turan. The Royal Commander of Guards does not go seeking trifles. But that is Nahdir's concern, not yours."

"Shir Khan's word is given," Mansouri said grudgingly. "Yet it would be a sign of better faith if he spread his goods willingly in front of us and let us see with our own eyes."

Some of the robbers scowled at this while others murmured agreement.

"Strip my tent?" Shir Khan burst out. "Search my garments? As well call me a liar!" Then he spat such curses that the face of Mansouri paled:

"I take those words from no man, not even the Lion of the World!"

"You will take them!" roared Shir Khan. "Take and choke on them!"

"And you, Lion, take this!"

Mansouri snatched out one of his daggers and plunged it to the hilt into Shir Khan's belly. For a moment, the robber chieftain stared at the blood staining his shirt. He plucked at the blade as if it were some vaguely puzzling object. His mouth went slack and he dropped to one knee.

One of the henchmen threw himself upon Mansouri and tried to grapple with him. But another sprang to defend his comrade. Mansouri at the same time broke free of his attacker. Joined by his comrade, they stood their ground against the others. Hard pressed, they soon gave way and took to their heels while the rest set after them.

The versifier ran to the horse lines, untethered the animals and sent them galloping in all directions. A ragged figure darted from the tent and threw himself in the path of Lukas.

It was a boy hardly taller than Lukas's belt and grubbier than Lukas had ever been at the same age. His long hair was clotted with mud, and the rest of him appeared to be mainly knees and elbows, scraped raw and overlaid with grime.

"What the devil—" cried Lukas.

The urchin grinned at him and studied him with gray eyes so round and large they seemed to eat up his whole face. "Do you think I am a devil? No, I am Haki. And I heard you call yourself al-Ukash. You did well. This Shir Khan is a bad one. He caught me in the hills two days ago, and thinks he will sell me for a slave. That is foolish. There is no good price now for Bishangaris."

Lukas noticed the boy's wrists were tied behind him. Taking out his knife, he cut the ropes. Haki stopped talking long enough to wipe his nose on the back of his hand.

By now, the versifier had returned. At sight of the boy, Kayim burst out laughing. "What have we here? An apprentice robber?"

When Lukas told him, the versifier clapped his hands to his head. "Not another Bishangari! We've already been diddled by one!"

"Oh, I will not diddle you," replied Haki. "You are

my benefactors. I am bound to you in honor, closer than blood brothers. I will stay with you, if you wish, forever."

"A simple thank-you will do," answered the versifier.

Lukas had gone to Shir Khan. The bandit lay on the turf, the look of bewilderment frozen across his face. Lukas turned away. "Kayim, I killed him as surely as if I'd stabbed him with my own hand."

"We'll end up the same way if we don't get moving. When those villains get tired of chasing each other, they'll be back for us. Let this ragamuffin find his way home. He's big enough to look after himself."

"Wait," said Lukas. He looked sharply at Haki. "You're bound to us in honor? Does that include guiding us into Bishangar?"

"That is correct, al-Ukash. I will take you wherever you wish to go. Only it is not such a wise thing to do."

"We have our reasons," Lukas said. "Important ones. There are lives at stake. Many of them. Yours, too, very likely. We have to find your King Ardashir."

Haki frowned. "This must be a great matter, al-Ukash. I know nothing of such things. But my brother Yussuf is clever. I will take you to my village."

"Will he help us?"

"Ah, he is not there now. My cousin Ibram is almost as clever. He is not there, either. But my uncle Sahlik will be grateful to you. They will all be grateful to you. Not my mother and father, I am sorry to say, they are dead.

You come with me. No one will harm you if I tell them not to."

Lukas climbed astride the pony. Haki sprang up behind him:

"These are not such good animals. I could have done better for you. It was foolish to chase away those horses. Your friend is perhaps not as clever as you. Is your ankle hurting? If you wish, I will see to it. Do you play chess, al-Ukash? My brother Yussuf taught me. I can make the board and pieces if you want to learn. Do you have any cheese? My Aunt Mariam makes excellent cheese. How old are you, al-Ukash? Does your friend never cut his moustache?"

"We might have come to grief because of a thief," muttered the versifier. "But this one's a mouth on two legs! If it eats as much as it chatters, we'll all starve to death."

CHAPTER

❦❦ *15* ❦❦

*D*uring the next several days, as they rode through the foothills toward the Mountains of Ramayan, the versifier's predictions showed every sign of coming true.

"How does he do it?" wailed Kayim. "I've never seen a human being talk and swallow his food at the same time. I could make a fortune with that imp, showing him off in the bazaar."

While Haki's chatter ended only when he occasionally slept, Lukas quickly recognized the value of listening to him. In addition to the boy's gossip about his countless uncles, aunts, and cousins, Lukas learned that Haki was only one of dozens who had made their way into Abadan to glean whatever news they could. Haki already knew more of Shugdad's plans than Lukas could have discovered on his own. The army had been raised; troops were in Jannat al-Khuld, where Shugdad himself had headquarters. The invasion of Bishangar could be launched at any time.

"Do not worry, al-Ukash," Haki told him. "My village is not far. You will see our goats. Are you fond of goats, al-Ukash? I like them better than sheep. Why does your friend always talk to himself? He does not seem happy in the mountains. Why does he call himself a versifier? His verses are not very good. Do you have a trade? Can you read? My Aunt Mariam taught me. She will make a feast for us. What do you like to eat?"

For all his happy rattling, at times his face would turn solemn and his eyes darken. Though Haki seemed devoted to his benefactors, Lukas could not rid himself of a suspicion that the boy was not telling all he knew.

"I should hope not," Kayim said when Lukas spoke to him of this. "I've heard enough about his goats, his relatives, and his brother Yussuf. Do you think he's up to something?"

Lukas shook his head. "It isn't that. I don't know what it is. Anyway, there's nothing we can do about it."

He said no more. One thing he did not doubt. Without the boy's help, they could never have come this far. He had never reckoned on such mountains. Alone, Lukas would have been lost from the first day he left the foothills and entered the Ramayan.

At first, he felt dwarfed by the peaks. Soon, he came to marvel at them. The heights held as many shapes in stone as the clouds above: the hulks of ships; tall, broken stairways; towers and belfries. Many of the slopes were awash in a tide of green-black vegetation. Cresting waves of woodlands broke against the hillsides, swirled through the valleys, then drained away to leave barren stretches of gravel and loose stones.

Nights were nearly as bright as the days. Huddled in his sheepskin against the chill, Lukas fancied all the Ramayan had been turned upside down and its gems shaken loose into the sky. "We are very close to the stars," Nur-Jehan had told him. He had laughed to himself then, disbelieving any difference between Abadani and Bishangari stars. But the girl had been right. Now he understood her impatience to return. He had been tempted to ask Haki if he knew of the girl. With the boy's inexhaustible supply of kinfolk, she could well be among them. But he said nothing. He did not want to think of her.

They had been gradually bearing east through the mountains for the past three days, with Haki on foot scrambling through the narrow defiles. Midmorning of the fourth day, the boy skittered ahead, leaped onto an outcropping of rocks, and pointed downward. Once sure Lukas had seen his signal, he raced out of sight.

Lukas put his pony into a trot. Against one wall of the valley rose a cluster of rough stone buildings, with sparse patches of grazing land on the slopes above. Haki had already reached one of the square, flat-roofed houses. From all directions, villagers ran to meet him. As

Lukas and Kayim drew closer, the versifier began counting off on his fingers:

"The big fellow with the red whiskers is Uncle Sahlik. The woman with the shawl over her head is Aunt
Mariam. The two goats are Taji and Raji. Taji's the black
one. Now, for the cousins—I swear, that imp has babbled so much I know them already."

Haki had exaggerated neither the gratitude nor the
welcome his benefactors would receive. His kinsmen,
who seemed to include most of the village, joined in setting out fragrant stews, jars of honey, and jugs of a con-
coction brewed by Uncle Sahlik himself. With all his
chattering, Haki had not mentioned one detail, perhaps
judging it less important than describing the livestock.
Sahlik, Lukas now learned, was the village chief and
head of the Council of Elders; a man of more weight and
authority than Haki had led Lukas to believe.

When the festivities ended, Sahlik drew Lukas aside
to speak alone with him. The boy, Lukas realized, had
already told the chieftain as much as he knew. Sahlik,
however, was not satisfied and he questioned Lukas with
great courtesy but also great shrewdness. Sahlik was a
broad, barrel-chested mountaineer, good-natured and
open-faced; yet there were moments when Lukas sensed
a fleeting somber glance. To gain the chieftain's trust,
Lukas decided he could tell the man no less than the
truth, who he was and what he intended to do.

Learning that his guest claimed to be none other than

the King of Abadan, Sahlik knit his brows and said nothing for a long while, studying Lukas closely.

"You ask my help," he finally said to Lukas. "I cannot give it or refuse it of my own accord. Such a decision is too heavy for one to bear alone. The Council shall meet. Among us, we shall agree on what must be done."

Lukas nodded. He could not reproach Sahlik's caution. He was troubled, however, at being forbidden to attend the meeting. Though he protested reasonably, and urged Sahlik to allow him to be present, the chieftain firmly refused. Sahlik did grant Lukas and the versifier the freedom of the village while the Council deliberated.

With his head likely hanging in the balance, Lukas had little heart to roam the village. Haki had vanished into the midst of his relatives, so Lukas and the versifier wandered cautiously on their own. To the astonishment of Lukas, every door was unlatched to them and his uneasiness changed to fascination.

The villagers greeted them openly and frankly. Lukas soon realized it was not their custom to stand on great ceremony. They were courteous and hospitable, simple and straightforward in all their ways.

"I'm beginning to think that girl of yours wasn't Bishangari at all," whispered Kayim. "She certainly didn't behave like these folk. Of course," he added, "for all we know, Sahlik and his friends may be deciding to skin us alive. If they do, I'm sure they'll be cordial about it."

Lukas tried to keep that thought from his mind, preferring to watch the rug weavers and the village goldsmith at work. Not even the treasures of the Shirazan Palace could match the beauty of the carpets and common household goods of these Bishangaris. Nur-Jehan had told him of precious stones, but he had never expected so many worn so casually on rings and brooches, necklaces and earrings. Seeing youngsters playing around a circle scratched in the dust, the versifier's eyes popped and he nudged Lukas:

"Those aren't bits of glass, my friend. These people have fortunes stuck in their ears or hanging around their necks. It means nothing to them!"

"It means their lives," Lukas answered bitterly. "Shugdad would cut their throats to get his hands on one bag of their marbles."

There were few young men and women in the village; but the two strangers quickly gained a following of boys and girls much the same age as Haki. The versifier, unable to resist an audience of any kind in any circumstances, squatted on a doorsill and trotted out some of his best tales. His listeners laughed and clapped their hands at the invisible camel.

"These Bishangaris!" The versifier beamed. "What intelligence! What marvelous taste and perception!"

No sooner did Kayim finish a tale than his listeners told one in return. The versifier admitted getting the better of the bargain.

"Their village tales are remarkable! I must try to remember them. Naturally, they need a little polishing and touching up. That's to be expected. These toddlers don't have the skill of a public versifier. But I'd be glad to stay here and collect a few dozen stories."

Lukas was about to ask one of the children to repeat her tale when he heard his name called from the doorway of Sahlik's house.

"If they aren't going to help us," said Kayim as they hurried to enter, "at least they could make us honorary Bishangaris."

In the largest chamber of the house, the men and women of the Council sat waiting around a low table. Lukas could read nothing in the faces turned toward him as he stood silently before them.

"You have called yourself King of Abadan," Sahlik began. "Word has already reached us that Shugdad rules, that Kasha is dead. Nevertheless, you claim to be the rightful King. You cannot prove this, nor can we disprove it. I say to you frankly that some of us do not believe you. We must allow, even so, the possibility that you are telling us the truth.

"Since that possibility exists, we are all agreed the risk is worth taking. If what you say is true, we have everything to gain: our land, our very lives. If what you say is false, we lose only what we might lose in any case. As for you, al-Ukash—or Kasha, King of Abadan—be assured of one thing beyond any doubt or question. If you are not dealing honestly with us, this will become known. You will not live past that moment.

"We cannot do all you ask. We can only help you by putting you in the hands of those who may help you further. We shall give you what you need to make your way there."

"Where would you have me go?" Lukas asked.

"That is not for you to know. You ask our trust. Then trust our judgment. It is safer for all if you do not know your destination. Haki will guide you. We can do no more. We can do no less. Go in peace. May your steps be fortunate."

Lukas thanked them and Sahlik rose and led him from the chamber. In the dooryard stood two fresh ponies, already saddled and laden with provisions. On a third perched Haki, grinning all over his face.

"I shall take you where you wish to go, al-Ukash. Did you think I would not stay with you? I am an excellent guide. Are you truly a king? You do not look much like one. Why did you change your name? I will call you al-Ukash, even so. I like that better. Do they have goats in Shirazan Palace? Hurry up, al-Ukash, they are all waiting to say farewell to us. Did you meet my cousin Hamid?"

The versifier rolled up his eyes. "I hope Sahlik knows what he's doing. It's bad enough sending us out in the charge of a boy. But all this prattling will set my wits rattling. I never thought silence could be a luxury."

Loose-tongued though he was, and willing to chatter about everything else under the sun, the boy said not a word to reveal their destination. Nor did Lukas try to winkle it out of him, sure it would be useless. As best he could judge, they were traveling eastward through the Ramayan, above Jannat. If Shugdad had taken the once-great city for his headquarters, it was a reasonable guess that King Ardashir might have disposed his own troops in the overlooking hills.

For the next two days, however, he saw nothing of Shugdad's armies or outposts. Nor was there any sign of Bishangari patrols. Haki assured him that they had probably chosen to keep out of sight. This only made the versifier more morose.

"I don't like the sensation," Kayim protested. "Who knows how many furious Bishangaris could be lurking among those rocks? They can see us, but we can't see them. Suppose they don't care for our looks? And come bucketing down on us? Our garrulous friend is going to have to talk faster than ever."

Not daring to build a fire, they ate their meals cold and hastily: a thick gruel of dark brown flour and strips of dried meat which the versifier eyed suspiciously.

"If this is what I think it is," groaned Kayim, "I'll be leaping from crag to crag, going beh-beh-beh! The only bleating public versifier in Abadan! Still, that wouldn't be much worse than some others I've heard."

At sundown, two slept while one stood guard. That night, Lukas had taken the last watch. Near dawn, he heard faint movements and what seemed the muffled whinny of a horse, close by a tumble of boulders.

He trod cautiously a few paces beyond a rock embankment. There was nothing. The mountains were playing tricks on his ears. The sound, he guessed, had come from a much greater distance. He gave a sigh of relief, glad that he had no cause to alarm his exhausted friends. He crept a little further down a gully. Past the angle of a sheer wall of stone, he suddenly halted. A huddle of men squatted by their horses. These were not hill folk but an Abadani mounted patrol.

He drew back hurriedly, only to plunge headlong against the studded jacket of an Abadani soldier. The trooper seized him and wrestled him to the ground, meanwhile calling for his comrades. Within the instant, the rest of the patrol fell upon him and dragged him to an open space where he was efficiently searched, his knife snatched from his belt; and he was hauled upright by the hair to face his captors.

"Well caught!" cried one. "A Bishangari goat! That's a good morning's work already. Watch your backs. There could be a herd of them."

"No Bishangari," said the trooper who had first laid hands on Lukas, "though he's dirty enough to be one."

"I've lost my company," Lukas put in. "I fell behind and I've been trying to catch up with them."

The burly trooper squinted at him. "Where's your kit? Your sword?"

"Gone. Lost when I pitched into a ravine."

"Liar. There's no company in these parts but us. You're a deserter, that's what you are."

"Cut his throat, and let's be on our way," urged one of the patrol. "If there's Bishangari here, I don't want them to find us, any more than I want to find them."

"He's no deserter," declared another, who wore the badge of an under-officer. "Can you see a deserter staying in these mother-forsaken rock piles? A spy, more likely."

"Cut his throat for spying, then."

The officer spat. "Your grandmother was a bow-legged camel. He's a liar, but you're a fool. We'll take him to Jannat. Do you want a better reason for coming in off patrol? Use your head and you won't have to wear out your backside. Mount up. Now you understand why I carry the rank and you'll sweep stables for the rest of the war."

CHAPTER
❧❧ 16 ❧❧

$\mathcal{G}$lad for any excuse to break off the patrol, the troopers quickly obeyed. Lukas was bound, hoisted up behind one of them, and the band set off at a trot down a narrow path.

Their direction took them further from Kayim and Haki, the only thing for which Lukas could be grateful. His friends were safe, the troopers suspected nothing. One moment, he hoped the versifier and the boy would try to free him; the next, he hoped they would not be so foolhardy. His mind raced from one plan to another, all impossible. At last, he let his head droop and gave up even imagining what would be done to him.

His captors, by contrast, were in high spirits. The horsemen laughed and joked among themselves, paying no more attention to Lukas than a side of beef. The prospect of shelter and a hot meal spurred them on. They seldom halted, and just before sundown galloped through the gates of Jannat al-Khuld.

Nur-Jehan had spoken of Jannat as once mightier and more beautiful than Shirazan. His glimpse of ruined turrets and broken spires let Lukas only guess what the city had been. Stripped of their paving, the wide avenues were choked with pack animals and columns of soldiers. Tents rose in what had been a spacious bazaar. Along fire-blackened walls, companies of spearmen had stacked their weapons and flung themselves down to drowse or gamble amid the baggage.

At last they halted before the crumbling archway of a weed-infested courtyard. Lukas was pulled from the saddle, hauled through the entry and down an arcade running the length of what must have been a garden, now marred by rubbish heaps.

For a while it seemed his captors would have more trouble disposing of him than seizing him in the first place. The couriers bustling in and out ignored the troopers. The clerks and scribes kept their noses in their papers, not deigning to glance at the intruders.

As a party of officers strode by, the patrol leader finally dared put himself in their path, saluting and calling out that a spy had been caught in the Ramayan.

One of the staff cursed at him and ordered him and his men back to their own commander. But the senior officer halted a moment and stepped closer to Lukas, who found himself face to face with Nahdir.

The Commander of Guards stared for several moments, then seized the patrol leader by the front of his jacket:

"Where was this dog taken? Have you questioned him? What has he said of himself?"

The under-officer began stammering a report, but Lukas broke in, looking straight at the Commander of Guards:

"You know me well enough, Nahdir Aga."

Nahdir struck him across the face. "This is a wanted criminal, a traitor to the King." Turning to the patrol leader, he said, "You and your men have done well. Wait in the courtyard. You will be rewarded."

Lukas, head ringing from the blow, was held by two guards and, with Nahdir following, dragged up a flight of steps and thrown into an empty chamber. No sooner was the door bolted behind him than he cast about for some escape. A window overlooked the courtyard, but an iron lattice blocked any passage. Bound as he was, Lukas could not even try to shake the grating loose. Even so, he feared the courtyard would be as much a trap as the chamber. In the fading light, he glimpsed a narrow ledge jutting below the lattice and seeming to run the length of the house. Once on the ledge, it might be barely possible to inch along to the end of the wall and from there drop into the street.

He could attempt nothing until his hands were free, so he flung himself down on a pile of carpets and began worrying at the ropes that bound him.

In a few moments, he was obliged to stop. The bolt

rattled as the door opened and a guard entered. Setting an oil lamp on the floor, he withdrew as a figure stepped from the shadows of the corridor.

Shugdad strode into the chamber. He was garbed in full military regalia. His gold breastplate shone against the crimson of his long cloak. A turban was wrapped around a close-fitting helmet. A sword in a gem-studded scabbard hung at his side. Shugdad's beard had been cropped short and it made his face look hammered out of iron.

Lukas, despite himself, felt a surge of fear at the sight of his former Grand Vizier. This man, he had to admit, had all the bearing of a king. Lukas stared, horrified and fascinated. For an instant, overwhelmed by the raw force of power, he would have risen to his feet had Shugdad so commanded.

The moment passed. Forcing himself to look Shugdad in the eyes, Lukas said, in as light a tone as he could manage, "Is it now custom, Shugdad Mirza, to come armed in the King's presence?"

"Were you a king," replied Shugdad, "even though captive, you would be paid due honor. You are no king and never were."

"Why, Shugdad," said Lukas, "it seems to me you were the first to hail me Center of the Universe. Predicted, prophesied—"

"The babblings of a foolish astrologer. A true king knows the nature of power, how to grasp it, how to wield it like a sword. You played with it like a child with a toy.

In the end, you let it slip from your fingers, and thus proved yourself unworthy to hold it."

"And you, Shugdad, are you worthy? There was a Bishangari slave who would have made a better ruler than either of us. But you're right in one thing. I was King by accident and never thought I'd be one for long. Even so, I doubt you'll serve your people much better than I did."

"Serve the people?" Shugdad looked scornfully at him. "The people serve the king. So it must be. You sought to rule by weakness instead of strength. Had I allowed it, I would have failed in my own duty. King Kasha! I took your measure from the first: a fool and a weakling. You should have had me slain while power still was yours. Had I been in your place, I would not have hesitated."

"You didn't hesitate long," answered Lukas. "You've already declared me dead. That was impatient of you."

"You have been misinformed," said Shugdad. "Your death was only presumed. The distinction is now trivial, since you will shortly be dead beyond presumption."

"Go away, Shugdad," Lukas said wearily. "You're going to kill me, but don't bore me to death."

"I came to offer you a last choice: an easy death or a difficult one."

Lukas grinned at him. "Do you have anything better?"

"You will regret your impudence when you are in the hands of Nahdir."

"So you're here to do me a favor. Out of the goodness of your heart, I'm sure."

"I require a document from you," said Shugdad. "A document written in your own hand, declaring that you sought to betray the kingdom; that you plotted with King Ardashir; then, in remorse, took your own life."

"Are you out of your wits? Being King must have gone to your head. You want me, seriously, to write such nonsense? Go forge your own scrap of paper, I'm sure you're capable of it. It will serve as well, for anyone fool enough to believe it in the first place."

"Such a writing is not absolutely essential," replied Shugdad. "Nevertheless, I would prefer to have it as a matter of evidence for the Royal Archives. A convenience, shall we say. With it or without, your treachery will be proved when your body is found in Bishangar."

"It will prove nothing. Anyone with common sense will guess the truth."

"The king who holds power over men also holds power over the truth. If it is not believed, it will nonetheless be accepted. It comes to the same thing."

"Some live who will justify me."

"Locman? He is known to be in Bayaz and will be dealt with. A public versifier? Wherever he may be, he will not live long. In any case, who will credit a mumbling dotard or a notorious thief and liar? The men who found you have already been put to death. If King Kasha is remembered at all, it will be only to curse his infamy."

"No," said Lukas. "Sooner or later, you'll be cursed more than I will."

"On my progress to Jannat, I passed through a certain town," said Shugdad. "In the bazaar, a horse was kept saddled and ready for the day King Kasha would return even from the dead.

"I commanded the animal's throat to be cut, and the carcass hung at the city gates. It shall be thus with any in Abadan who hope so foolishly."

"If you're so shaken by a horse, what next? Will you butcher camels and jackasses?" Lukas threw back his head and burst into laughter. "I can't believe it! Poor man, you're afraid of me! I gave you more credit than you deserved. When I saw you just now, I really took you for a king. A bad one, but a king nevertheless. For all your trappings, the more I see of you, you're worse than a pettifogging notary with your plots and documents and cheap-jack schemes. You're as noble as my town barber, and he's better suited to his trade of bleeding and leeching than you to yours. And to cap it all, you'll keep on being afraid of me even after I'm dead."

Shugdad stiffened. His face had gone pale. Lukas thought the man would draw sword and cut him down in that instant. Shugdad regained his composure and strode to the door. There he halted, and said quietly, "Believe one thing. You will die very badly."

CHAPTER

❧❧ *17* ❧❧

*A*nd that," groaned Lukas, "is the truest thing I've heard from Shugdad." He climbed to his feet. "As for Battisto, he's played a marvelous trick on me." Rage growing faster than his despair, he stumbled to the lattice. "Can you hear me, you skinny little wretch, wherever you are?" He battered his shoulders against the iron. "Is this what you had up your sleeve for me? Is this good sport for you? To the devil with you, if you aren't there already!"

He succeeded only in bruising his bones. At least somewhat relieved by his outburst, he turned his efforts again to loosening his bonds. Lukas, who prided himself on undoing any knot, found his fingers numb and useless. He kept on, nevertheless, more to occupy his time than with any real hope of getting free.

He left off as soon as he heard sounds at the door.

The guard admitted two servants: one bearing a basin of food; the other, a water jug.

"Welcome," said Lukas, pumping up the bravado remaining to him. "Whatever else King Shugdad has in mind, he won't starve me to death. Be good fellows and untie me, unless you want the trouble of feeding me."

The servant set down the jug and came to do his bidding. Between the man's greasy headcloth and the scarf half-covering his face, Lukas glimpsed the twin branches of a moustache. He choked back a glad cry.

"Keep your voice down," warned Kayim. "I told your guard we'd been ordered to bring you food. As things go in the army, he's too confused to know whether it's true or not. But I don't dare stay. The oaf saw two of us come in, and he can surely count high enough to see whether two of us come out."

"Where's Haki? Is he safe?"

"Safe and happy in the kitchen," said Kayim, unbinding Lukas, whose astonishment grew at the sight of the other servant suddenly kneeling and kissing the ground before him. It was Namash, the water seller.

"What's this?" gasped Lukas. "What are you doing here? Get up, man! How did you—?"

"Center of the Universe," replied Namash, "your friend told me everything. King of Abadan! How could I have known? Wonder of the Age, I can tell you that you made a first-rate beggar."

"Haki and I followed the patrol," put in Kayim. "We

[155]

sneaked into the kitchen. They're all in such an uproar trying to serve Shugdad, I thought two more servants wouldn't be noticed. Then we stumbled into our friend here."

"What, Namash, have you turned cook and given up the victualing trade?"

"Added to it," answered Namash. "I deal in carpets, shawls, lambskins. Since the day you sent me that purse of gold—yes, I know about that, too—I've had nothing but good luck. This house is mine, bought outright. The finest in Jannat, or so it must have been in the old days. What else would Shugdad take for his headquarters? But who cares about that? We have to get you out of here."

A low whistle came from the lattice. Lukas spun around to see what appeared to be an enormous bat clinging to the grillwork.

"Do not trouble yourself, al-Ukash," whispered Haki. "It was not clever of you to be caught by those Abadanis, but we are all together again, and you will be free very soon."

"Imp!" cried the versifier. "I told you to stay in the kitchen and wait for us. All right, since you're there: how strong are those bars?"

"Very strong. They will not bend even a little."

"If we could get hold of a saw," said Kayim, going to examine the lattice, "or a file, and cut through—"

"Won't do," put in Namash. "It would take too long. The noise—they'd be on to us in a minute."

"You're right." The versifier sighed. "Well, then, suppose I stayed here? Let al-Ukash—the King, that is —let him put on my clothes, take the water jug—"

"No," said Lukas. "Neither one of you will take my place. If Shugdad finds you here instead of me, he'll kill you."

"He's been wanting to do that for some time," said Kayim. "I admit I don't like putting opportunity in his way. But as it stands, he's bound to get one of us. Un-less—" The versifier snapped his fingers. "Unless you were already dead. I mean, if he thought you were."

Lukas shook his head. "There's no way to make him believe that."

"There is," Kayim insisted. "We send Haki to an apothecary for a drug, some kind of potion. Strong enough to put you so fast asleep they'll take you for dead. Namash offers to bury you—which, of course, he doesn't. But we trundle you out of here, bring you back to your senses. And there you are!"

"That's madness!" cried Lukas. "There's no way it could work. You won't fool Shugdad so easily with a sham corpse. We'd soon be real ones."

"The King is right," said Namash. "There's a risk every step of the way."

"A very foolish plan—" Haki began.

"Don't rattle at me, I'm only trying to think of some-thing, no matter what," protested the versifier. "There's a tale I tell, where a princess takes a sleeping potion. Alas, I have to agree with you. It's a fine tale so long as you don't look at it too closely, or ask embarrassing questions. No, I admit it won't answer at all."

The versifier broke off as the guard unbolted the door. The man thrust in his head and ordered the servants to have done and report to the kitchen.

"We'll come back as soon as we can," whispered Kayim, replacing the cords so that Lukas could pull free of them. Haki had vanished. The versifier hurried after Namash.

With his friends near, Lukas's spirits rose a little. But he still had no better hope for escape. He shut his eyes and tried to sleep. Only able to drowse, he started up instantly when the bolt rattled.

It was not Kayim, but Nahdir. Lukas struggled to hide his panic. They had all forgotten one thing that turned every scheme useless. Shugdad would act at *his* convenience, not theirs.

"Get up," ordered the Commander of Guards. "You are to be taken from here into the Ramayan."

"You'd have me walk to my own funeral?" Eyes fixed on Nahdir, Lukas slipped his hands free of the ropes. A sharp odor was filling his nostrils. The stench of his own fear, thought Lukas, nevertheless staring insolently at the Commander of Guards. "Well, you can go to the devil before I move a step. If you want me in Bishangar, you'll have to drag me there."

Splotches broke out on Nahdir's face, but he held himself tightly in check. Though his fingers twitched, his hand stayed from his sword.

"Call your guards," said Lukas. "They'll do it if you can't." The stench had grown stronger, catching at his throat. It was not his imagination. Nahdir, too, had noticed it.

The door flung open as the guard burst into the chamber:

"Fire! Nahdir Aga, the house is burning!"

No sooner had the guard bawled his warning than he pitched senseless to the floor, felled by Kayim, who had swung an iron cook pot down on his head. Haki darted past the versifier.

Nahdir gave them no more than a glance. Instead of facing the intruders, he snatched out his sword and leaped forward to strike at Lukas.

As the Commander of Guards brought up his weapon, Lukas sprang aside. He seized the burning oil lamp and flung it squarely into Nahdir's face. The man roared and clutched at his eyes. His beard shot up in flames. In another moment, the spattering oil set his cloak and turban ablaze.

"Out! Into the street!" shouted Kayim, flung against the wall as Nahdir, pain-maddened, plunged through the doorway. With Haki and the versifier at his heels, Lukas raced from the chamber. The Commander of Guards had hurtled down the stairs into the press of staff officers and soldiers, spreading flame wherever he passed.

Lukas thought he heard Shugdad's voice from the upper floor, but the Vizier's shouted commands were lost in the commotion. The crowd was streaming into the courtyard. He glimpsed Namash, who gestured for the three to follow him down a flight of wooden steps into a cellar storeroom. There, smoke rose in such clouds that Lukas could barely see. What he did see he could not believe. The water seller, instead of beating out the flames, was feeding them with all the burnable household goods he could lay hands on.

"Go!" cried Namash. "Through that door. To the end of the passage."

Lukas tried to pull him from the blaze, but Namash tore away:

"Be gone! Quick! Or I'll have set my house alight for nothing!"

"You? Burned your own house? Namash—"

"Don't yammer at me, King of Abadan. All I have came from you. I'm only giving it back." He shoved Lukas after Kayim and Haki, who had ducked through the door and were already in the street.

The fire had brought onlookers, soldiers, and townsfolk to Shugdad's headquarters. The fugitives threaded their way through the crowd as fast as they dared without calling attention to themselves.

Lukas was still bewildered at Namash sacrificing all his house and goods. "The man's ruined himself for me. I never said so much as a thank-you."

"Hardly the moment for it," answered Kayim. "He's quite a fellow, Master Namash. He'll manage, one way or another."

As the ponies had been abandoned, Lukas weighed

the risk of stealing mounts from the army horse lines.

"It won't be easy," warned the versifier. "Haki and I saw patrols and roadblocks all around. We don't know if Shugdad got out of the fire. With his devil's luck, we'll have to assume he did."

"No matter what," said Lukas, "we can't stay in Jannat. Haki should know a way." He stopped short. "Where is he?"

There was no sign of the boy who had been at their side a few moments before.

"He can't be far. Come on, we have to find him."

No sooner had Lukas begun retracing his steps than a beggar shambled up beside him, a big, lurching man covered in layer on layer of rags, who caught hold of Lukas's jacket and wailed for alms. In vain, Lukas protested that neither had one coin between them.

The beggar only clung more tightly as his whining grew more indignant, "Charity, masters! You take me for some bazaar scrounger? Cheated out of a fortune—" The man broke off. Thrusting a jowly, stubbly face closer to Lukas, he squinted and muttered, "I've seen you before, somewhere. As I never forget a horse, I never forget a face."

Lukas recognized Katir only an instant before the horse trader recognized him.

"You!" Katir bellowed. "You! Cheat! Robber!" Bawling curses and insults, the horse trader flung himself on Lukas. The versifier laid hold of Katir and tried to pull him away, and soon all three were battling.

Katir's shouting and scuffling had, meanwhile, drawn the attention of a patrol of military constables, who ran to look into the disturbance.

"Lock him up, officers!" cried Katir. "My horses were talking to him, but he lied to me."

The chief of the constables laughed. "Talking horses? That's one charge I've never heard. You're the one I should take in for being drunk or mad."

"Talked to him!" Katir insisted. "Told him where the treasure was. I couldn't understand them. Because of the accent, you see. But this wretch, he knows their language. One rawboned villain gave him some cock-and-bull tale about living in the palace. But I knew that one was lying. The mare found a dagger, though."

As Katir babbled on, the patrol chief glanced at his men and tapped a finger against his temple.

He turned to Katir.

"So your horses talk, do they? And camels read and write. Of course they do. I had a letter from one the other day. Written on the sole of a boot. Now, if you'd like to read that letter—"

"No, no, wait!" cried Katir. "There's more to it—"

"Yes, and more than enough," answered the chief.

He seized the protesting Katir and with a kick sent him scrambling away. "As for these two," he said, eyeing Lukas and Kayim, "they're out of uniform, if they had any to begin with. They're either deserters or trying to dodge the recruiting officers. To the lockup with them and we'll find out."

Lukas, heart in his mouth, glanced at the versifier. Kayim, he knew, was also calculating their chances of escape. At the same time, the squad groaned loudly at the orders of their chief. Some complained of the long march to the military jail at the far side of Jannat. Others urged simply killing the suspects out of hand.

The chief rubbed his jaw. "Yes, it would save making out a report. And come to the same thing in the end, as they'd be stuck up on spears one way or the other. Too good for them, as I see it. They'd be out of this mess once and for all, and the rest of us in it still. A waste, besides. We'll need every man against those Bishangari devils, so why throw these two away? No. Here's what I say, and if we all keep our mouths shut, there's none the wiser. Captain Dakkah's company's moving into the Ramayan. He'll be glad for all the men he can get, even these two, and no questions asked. Hustle them along.

Turn them over to Dakkah and we're in the clear."

The versifier's face had grown intensely thoughtful, which Lukas took to mean that Kayim was ready to escape then and there. Lukas gave a quick shake of his head. The patrol's laughter and nudgings that greeted their chief's decision had put Lukas on his guard. Captain Dakkah's company evidently had a bad reputation among the troops.

Nevertheless, when he and Kayim were ordered to fall in with the constables, he managed to whisper to the versifier, "Haki's quick-witted enough to take care of himself. I'll miss my guess if he isn't following us right now."

"Likely so," agreed Kayim. "I trust him to land on his feet no matter what. Yes, he'll be all right. I hate to admit it, but I miss the little rogue."

"Meantime, we've got a way out of Jannat," said Lukas. "Where's the last place Shugdad will look for us? In his own army. Two common soldiers. Not very enjoyable, but practical."

"Common is all well and good; it's the soldier part I don't care for," muttered Kayim. "The military life never tickled my fancy. Frankly, I'd rather versify battles than fight them. The battles come out bravely, the versifier comes out safely, and everyone's happy all around."

Quick-marched through the town, they soon reached the gate of Jannat. As Lukas had hoped, they passed through with no more challenge than an exchange of rough jokes between the watchmen and the constables.

From there, they were led among the troops encamped by the north wall, at last halting where a company of some hundred soldiers were striking tents and loading pack mules.

A grizzled, heavy-set trooper, with a grimy cloak on his shoulders, took them in charge. He seemed as glad to have the two reinforcements as the constables were to be rid of them. He rummaged through a pile of gear, pulling out two scabbardless blades and two small, dented shields, which he tossed to Lukas and the versifier.

Lukas had expected to be taken before Captain Dakkah. When he asked about this, the trooper, who gave his name as Hassan, only laughed.

"Dakkah was killed on the first sortie into the Ramayan. We don't let on, and keep drawing his rations. We still come out short of food, as you'll see. What have you two done? You don't have to answer. We mind our own business here."

Seeing the puzzled frown on Lukas's face, Hassan squinted at him.

"You don't know? They didn't tell you?" Hassan struck his hands together and burst out laughing again. "You poor, miserable lumps! Dakkah's Company? Dead Man's Company! We're a punishment troop. Sorties, patrols in force, whatever the commander thinks is worst. We're the point of the lance, and the army won't shed many tears if the point gets itself broken off.

"Don't worry about it. You've got a better chance here than being impaled on a spear, after a court martial.

There was so much of that—you'd get a death sentence if you sneezed crossways—the commander decided it was a waste of warm bodies. He figures why execute our own men. Let the Bishangaris do it. So he formed the punishment companies. Whatever you've done, you'll find plenty who did the same: deserters, insubordinates, a lot who were too fond of King Kasha and were fool enough to say so out loud."

When Lukas asked if he was now the company's officer, Hassan grinned and shook his head:

"Not me. That's a job nobody wants. The captain's at the head of the column somewhere. You'll find him soon enough. A good fellow, but a madman. But, then, so are all of us."

A bugle sounded, thin and piercing in the night chill. The column had formed and begun to move. Hassan ordered Lukas and Kayim to fall in with the others, then hurried off to round up stragglers and kick them into line.

The company set off at a dogtrot until well out of Jannat and the broken ground slowed their pace. From the first, Kayim had been groaning and sighing and lamenting the weight of his weapons. Lukas, too, was hard put to keep up with the company.

"The Royal Minister of Supply must give out special swords to the army," said Lukas. "The longer you carry them, the heavier they get. I wish I'd known that when I was in the palace; I'd have passed a law against it."

He had hoped for a signal from Haki, but none came. "I'm sure he knows where we are," Lukas insisted. "He's probably tagging along out of sight, laughing his head off at us. When the company's deeper into the mountains, that will be our best moment to escape."

"It can't be too soon for me," answered Kayim. "My blisters are big enough to march by themselves."

Lukas, meantime, had struck up an easy comradeship with the troopers. Convinced they were facing certain death, the soldiers gave themselves over to reckless high spirits, laughing and making sport of their predicament. The versifier did not find this reassuring.

"Hassan was right. They're all crazy. These maniacs are likely to do anything. Even fight!"

There was still no sign of Haki. Lukas admitted he was now seriously worried. "If I was wrong, if he's caught somewhere or lost track of us, we'll have to set off on our own."

"That's bad enough," said Kayim. "But Shugdad's going to start his attack. When he does, the Bishangaris won't be sitting on their hands. Then the fat will be in the fire. Even if you find Ardashir, it will be too late."

Lukas did not answer, unwilling to admit to himself that the versifier was probably right.

The company had halted. The men took no pains to post guards, nor did they hesitate to start cook fires. Since the Bishangaris surely knew their position already, they saw no use in missing a hot meal.

Lukas caught sight of one man sitting apart, a sheepskin vest thrown over his bare back. What he had first thought were shadows, Lukas realized were scars and gouges covering the man's arms. Guessing that this was the troop captain, and recalling Hassan's words, Lukas was curious to see who would accept to lead such a desperate command. He drew closer.

The man was blowing at the embers of his fire. As he raised his head, Lukas fell back, hand on his sword. Despite the broken features and the livid weal tracking across the ravaged face, Lukas knew him instantly. There was no likelihood he would ever forget the one who had come to strangle him in Shirazan Palace.

Hearing the stifled gasp, Osman instantly turned his eyes toward Lukas, stared dumbfounded a moment, then sprang to his feet. Too late to escape recognition, Lukas could only stand his ground. He snatched out his sword.

Osman made no attempt to draw his own blade. He strode up to Lukas, who held him off at sword's length.

"One word, Osman, and I swear I'll do what I should have done to you in the palace."

"Yes, as you should have done," Osman replied quietly. "Use your weapon, King of Abadan. This is the only favor I ask. I betrayed you once. I will not betray you a second time."

Though Osman spoke in a low voice, his tone was such that Lukas lowered the blade, uncertain what the man intended. Kayim had now come up.

At sight of the former palace guard, the versifier

burst out, "Traitor! Assassin! What are you doing among your betters? The worst rogue here is less a villain than you. It's bad enough scraping through these hills. Now we have a vicious dog leading the pack!"

Osman stood unmoving. "Say what you will. Hear me first."

"Let him tell us what he has to tell," Lukas said to the versifier. He gestured for Osman to follow him to the edge of the camp where they would not be overheard.

"I'm not interested," said Kayim. "The only thing I want to know is why Shugdad didn't execute him for bungling."

"I asked nothing better," said Osman. "When I understood the truth, that Shugdad sought only power for himself and not the good of the kingdom, I wished to die. I had betrayed the true King. Death would have been a kindness. Therefore, Shugdad denied it to me. Nahdir flogged me and when he wearied, Shugdad himself plied the lash. I was then condemned to serve in Dakkah's troop. We were sent to Jannat, and when Dakkah was slain, I accepted to lead his men."

"You've been lucky, anyway," said Lukas. "You could have been killed a dozen times over."

Osman looked squarely at him. "O King, you have not understood. I wished to die. My misfortune is that I still live. I have led sorties, fought hand to hand, thrown away my weapons and stood unarmed. My life is cursed, for I cannot lose it."

Osman unsheathed his knife and held it out to Lukas.

"King of Abadan, for the sake of my honor, do what you should have done long since."

"That's not honor, that's vanity," returned Lukas. "Or feeling sorry for yourself. One's as bad as the other. I don't need you dead. I need you very much alive. I also need you to keep your mouth shut. As far as your men are concerned, I'm al-Ukash, not King of Abadan."

"Declare yourself to them," replied Osman. "I can vouch for my company. If they know King Kasha lives, they will follow wherever you command."

"I wish I knew 'wherever,'" said Lukas. "That's the trouble." He hesitated a moment and then, despite Kayim's frown of disapproval, spoke plainly to Osman, holding back nothing of his plan.

"Time is against you," Osman said, when Lukas finished. "Yet I see no other hope. In any case, you are safer with us than alone in the Ramayan. Let this company be your bodyguard as long as you choose."

"The main thing," said Kayim, "is to stay clear of Bishangari troops."

Osman shook his head. "On the contrary, we must find them for you and draw them out, even if we let them attack us."

"What?" cried Kayim. "Put our heads in the lion's mouth?"

"There's nothing else we can do," said Lukas, ruefully adding, "except hope the lion doesn't bite down too hard."

Osman kept his word and gave no hint that Lukas was other than a common soldier in his company. Lukas, however, began to despair of drawing out Ardashir's troops. For two days, the company probed deeper into the mountains, bearing in the direction of the heights of Umm al-Raas. At times, they entered villages only to find them abandoned.

By now, the main body of Shugdad's army had entered the Ramayan. From the dust rising in the valley behind them, Lukas judged the advance guard already close. He had no choice but to urge Osman to press on as quickly as he could.

The company had halted near a stretch of gravel-strewn turf. As the bugle sounded the advance and the men straggled into line, there came sudden, fearsome shouts.

Within the instant, the empty crags sprang to life with bowmen, arrows on string. From a defile burst a troop of horsemen, swords drawn.

The company fell back. Kayim seized Lukas and tried to pull him to the cover of the rocks. Lukas twisted free and ran straight for the leader, whose steed was plunging recklessly forward. The rider, head bound in a scarf streaming to the wind, rose up in the stirrups, then drew rein so sharply the white stallion sank to its haunches.

"Nur-Jehan!" cried Lukas. "Nur-Jehan!"

Nur-Jehan threw back her cloak, took a silver bugle from her belt and blew a shrill signal. The riders checked their steeds. Among the troop, Lukas saw a number of women astride the mountain ponies. Armed like the men, they were garbed in sheepskins or lengths of coarse wool. In the ranks of the bowmen, he sighted half-grown boys and girls bearing the same weapons as their elders.

Rakush stamped and snorted as the girl sprang down from the saddle.

She took a step toward Lukas. "Well met, King of Abadan."

"Well met, is it?" Lukas retorted. "Another minute and you and your friends would have cut us to ribbons. I should have known, if ever a band of wild maniacs came pelting down on me, who'd be at the head of them! Will you put away that sword! And make those youngsters loosen their bowstrings before somebody gets hurt."

Nur-Jehan was about to reply, but Lukas hurried on, "And something else: Where's my dagger? You could have left me that, at least, when you went sneaking off without so much as a word. I thought we were friends. All your prattle about honor and nobility—well, my girl, I say that's a shabby way of showing it."

Nur-Jehan's eyes blazed and color sprang to her cheeks. "The King of Abadan speaks without understanding. I could not have done otherwise."

By now, with Osman following, Kayim had come to the side of Lukas. Seeing Nur-Jehan, the versifier clapped hands to his head: "For days, we go without glimpsing hide nor hair of a Bishangari! And the first we find—"

Osman had been staring at Nur-Jehan and at last recognized her. "The slave girl."

"No slave then, and no slave now," declared Nur-Jehan. She turned to Lukas. "I learned you were in the Ramayan. I was not told that the King marched with his own assassin."

"That's my concern, not yours," replied Lukas. "I must find Ardashir and talk about a peace treaty. Do you know where he is? Can you take me to him?"

"That is not possible," said Nur-Jehan.

"How not?" Lukas burst out. "Don't play games with me. Somebody knows where he is if you don't. There must be something you can do besides whooping and galloping and waving that sword."

"There is," answered the girl. "You shall come with me."

"I'll come, too," put in Kayim, "I'm Grand Vizier now, I'll have you know."

The girl nodded. "Very well. But for the rest, they are Abadani soldiers. We can neither guard them nor travel with them."

"You don't give yourself much choice," returned Lukas. "Yes, they're Abadanis, which makes them my subjects. I'm responsible for them and I won't see them come to harm."

"That is not for you to say. You are in our land now."

"I don't call a massacre very hospitable."

"We are not hospitable with our enemies."

Lukas turned to Osman. "Now, I think, you'd better tell the company who I am and what I'm trying to do. If they accept my command, let them swear they will harm no Bishangari. Tell them I pledge my own life on that."

Then, to Nur-Jehan, he said, "Your people must also be told why I'm here. If they agree, let them promise safety for my men."

The girl hesitated a moment, then turned and strode back to the horsemen, who dismounted and gathered around her. At her signal, the bowmen, weapons still at the ready, came to join the others.

Osman, meantime, had returned to the company. At the distance, Lukas could not make out his words and only watched uneasily as the men clustered around their captain. Then he heard his name shouted as Osman came forward and threw his sword to the ground.

Nur-Jehan, too, had come back; though before she

reached him, Lukas saw the Bishangaris loosen their bows and lower their short-bladed swords.

"We accept a truce," the girl said, "but only with your company."

Lukas took the hand she offered. "I'm sorry I said what I did. I never thought we'd meet again. Sometimes, though, I'd imagine what it would be like if we ever did see each other. But it's not easy to be friendly with a troop of cavalry galloping down on you."

"The blame is not yours. There was much you did not know. You shall learn these things now."

The versifier and Osman had joined them. "It's true," said Lukas, "Kayim's my Grand Vizier. And if that's to be my army back there, I name Osman Commander, General-in-Chief, and, for that matter, all the rest of my Council of War."

Nur-Jehan had led them through the rocky pass into a little clearing where pack animals and remounts stood tethered, cropping at the lean turf. Lukas gave a cry of astonishment. On top of a pile of baggage sat Haki, grinning from ear to ear.

"It is pleasant to see you again, al-Ukash. And the Grand Vizier Kayim, also. Who is the big Abadani with you? Oh, yes, it is the company officer. Very good. Now we are all happy and friendly together."

The boy jumped down and ran to them. Lukas clapped him on the shoulder. "I knew you'd turn up sooner or later, but I never thought you'd be in the Bishangari cavalry."

"You imp," Kayim put in, "how did you ever find us?"

"I never lost you," said Haki. "I was following all along. I saw you with the Abadanis. I thought it was better for me to go ahead and bring my friends to you. You were going the way I would have led you anyhow. Now all is well. My Uncle Sahlik will be happy to know al-Ukash is what he said. If al-Ukash had lied, that would have been unpleasant for everyone."

With that, Haki pulled a long knife from his boot. Lukas laughed at him. "Unpleasant to say the least of it. If I hadn't been King of Abadan, would you really have used that on me?"

"Oh, no, al-Ukash," protested Haki. "Never! I could not do such a thing to my benefactor. No, I would find someone else to do it. This is my weapon. I am now a Bishangari soldier. I cannot go back to my village, so I will stay with you as always. I tend the horses and am very busy, but we will have good times, even so. My brother Yussuf will be proud of me. Have I told you about my brother Yussuf?"

"Stop, stop!" cried the versifier, putting his fingers in his ears. "I'm happy to see you, but I'd be happier if you'd plug that leak. You're going to use up all your words before you're full grown."

Nur-Jehan motioned for them to sit. "Osman shall inform his men after we have talked. First, you shall hear me and understand what I tell you."

The girl was silent a moment, then looked squarely at

Lukas and said, "I cannot take you to King Ardashir. He is dead, killed in battle years ago."

Lukas frowned, puzzled. Neither Kayim nor Osman spoke. Nur-Jehan glanced at them and turned her eyes again to Lukas.

"We guard this secret with our lives. Indeed, our lives depend on it. I have told you of King Neriman, and told you that Ardashir was as great a king. The Abadanis feared him above all others. Had his death become known to them, had the Kings of Abadan ever realized they would not have to face him in battle, nothing would have held them in check.

"Ardashir is dead. Yet, for that very reason, he can be said to live. Since his death, rumors were spread among the Abadanis that he could be anywhere and everywhere in Bishangar: in the north, the south, among the crags of Umm al-Raas, in the hills above Jannat.

"Unable to find him, to engage him face to face, the Kings of Abadan came to fear him all the more. He could move swiftly, conceal himself as if he had powers of invisibility. The Kings of Abadan convinced themselves of these things and more, better than the Bishangaris could have done. The Kings of Abadan shaped their enemy in their own minds. They saw Ardashir as ruthless, cunning, unyielding. They did not realize they saw him only in the mirror of themselves. Alas, there was one thing they could not see: that there might ever be peace between our kingdoms."

Lukas drew a long breath, and shook his head in

wonder. "What a ruse! But even without King Ardashir, someone must be in command and must be brilliant at it. To hold Bishangar together, to rule it—whoever managed that has to be greater than Ardashir himself. Yes, he's the one I'm looking for. Is there no way you can take me to him?"

"Him?" A slight smile played on the girl's lips. "It is I. King Ardashir was my father. I am Nur-Jehan, Queen of Bishangar."

CHAPTER
❧ 20 ❧

My father died when I was barely half-grown," the girl went on. "It fell upon me, his daughter, to learn all that he had known, to be Queen in my own right, to command in the field, to rule my people wisely. It was I who ordered his death kept secret, for I understood the disaster that would overtake us if word of it came to Abadan. I went among the villages, to make sure that every Bishangari knew what was at stake. As I vowed to serve them, so they vowed to keep the secret. They have not broken their word.

"Now do you understand, Lukas-Kasha, what I dared not tell you? I do not blame you for thinking of me as you did. Do you imagine it cost me no pain?"

Lukas bowed his head. "I did have some hard words to say about you." Then he grinned at her. "But on our way to Turan, I began thinking you could rule a kingdom better than I could. It turns out I was right, at least in that."

"You give yourself less than you deserve," replied Nur-Jehan. "You helped me without knowing who I was, without thanks, without realizing how much I owed you.

"And you did what others failed to do. After I was captured, many of my people went searching for me. Even the most fearless and shrewdest tracker in the kingdom."

"That is me!" broke in Haki, who had been sitting cross-legged for a remarkably long period of silence. "You did my work for me, al-Ukash. But I could have found the Queen myself if it had not been for those bandits."

"I'm sure you could," said Lukas. "If you'd reached Shirazan, you'd have talked the palace walls down."

Nur-Jehan ordered her troop and the Abadani company to assemble and make their way to Umm al-Raas. Given one of the remounts, Lukas rode beside the girl at the head of the column.

"What a trick you played on me," he told her. "That beats any of mine. In Turan, you were ready to storm the place single-handed to get Rakush. I thought I could teach you something. I see I didn't need to."

"Not so, Lukas-Kasha. Do you believe I learned nothing from you? Had it not been for you, I could not have made my way to Bishangar.

[180]

"When I needed food and shelter, for Rakush more than myself, I found many in Abadan who were open-handed. Though most could guess I was a Bishangari, it made no difference to them. But others ill-treated me. I wanted to fight them to the knife for the sake of my honor. Yet each time, I heard you tell me that staying alive should be honor enough. So I held my tongue and my temper.

"I begged alms in the bazaar, groomed horses and swept stables, and put my hand to every menial task. I admit it stung my pride. You would have called it false pride. If lost, it was well lost. I traveled lighter without the burden of it. Yes, Lukas-Kasha, you taught me much, and better than you knew."

Before Nur-Jehan could say more, a courier, a girl of Haki's age, galloped to meet her. The message she carried urged the Queen's party to make all haste. The chief officers and the War Council had already gathered in their stronghold on the heights of Umm al-Raas.

For the rest of that day, the Queen of Bishangar led her troops higher into the mountains. Lukas had named Hassan captain of his own company now that Osman served as General-in-Chief; and for a time the Abadanis kept to themselves. As progress along the trails grew more difficult, tempers flared between the two parties and Lukas feared the truce might shatter. During a halt, an Abadani soldier and one of Nur-Jehan's horsemen fell to quarreling so hotly that knives were drawn.

The two were at last disarmed and dragged, still shouting curses at each other, before Lukas and Nur-Jehan. The Abadani was one of Hassan's best men, and he demanded punishment for the Bishangari, though none could be certain who had begun the quarrel.

"He called us filthy camels," declared Hassan. "We all heard him."

"And us?" cried the Bishangari officer. "They called us evil-smelling goats!"

Nur-Jehan's eyes flashed. "You were commanded to keep peace with each other. Both have disobeyed—"

Lukas drew the girl aside before she could finish, and whispered in her ear, "Have a care, Queen of Bishangar. Judge carefully or you'll do more harm than good."

"This judgment is simple," Nur-Jehan retorted. "Your officer wishes to protect his man at our expense. This will not be accepted. He must be punished, and set an example."

"Your own officer's doing the same thing," said Lukas.

"Then let them both be whipped in equal measure."

"You'll end up with worse than a pair of raw backs," Lukas said. "Punish them like that, and both companies will be at each other's throats more than ever. Were you so quick-tempered when you were sweeping stables? Now, Queen of Bishangar, if you'll permit a suggestion—"

The girl listened, at first reluctantly, as Lukas went

on. Then she nodded her head. Returning to the culprits and their officers, she declared:

"The King of Abadan and I have agreed on this matter. It is claimed that insults were exchanged between you. But is this in fact the case?

"The camel is a beast of strength, patience, and endurance. How, then, can it be an insult to be called one? The goat is agile and daring and, beyond that, provides milk and cheese. This is a creature to be honored and admired. We find, therefore, that you have in no way insulted each other. On the contrary, you have paid each other the highest compliments."

"As for filthy and evil-smelling," put in Lukas, "if you all stand a little downwind from one another, you'll realize very quickly that's a simple statement of fact."

"Since you have paid tribute to each other's admirable qualities," said Nur-Jehan, "there is only cause for praise, not punishment. Henceforth, the Bishangaris shall proudly call themselves 'The Queen's Own Goats,' and the Abadanis, 'The King's Royal Camels.'"

"And when you have the chance," added Lukas, "you might all do some scrubbing."

From that day, the same hardships that had rubbed both companies raw began to heal them. A rough joke that once would have brought blades flashing, now brought only laughter. The more outrageous the banter, the more their friendship grew.

"I still have much to learn," Nur-Jehan admitted.

"Keep working at it," replied Lukas. "With patience and application, you could be as much a rogue as your teacher."

Umm al-Raas rose highest of all peaks in Bishangar. When at last they reached its summit, Nur-Jehan led them into the deepest cavern Lukas had ever seen. Seeming to stretch for miles, it was honeycombed with chambers and hallways: some natural, others hewn from the living rock. Gems studded many of the rough walls; and even the flicker of an oil lamp set them sparkling so brilliantly that Lukas had to turn his eyes away.

"So this is what Shugdad's after." Lukas grimaced. "On top of everything else, he's a fool. He's greedy for treasure because it's scarce, but there're so many gems here they'd end up worth nothing at all. The boys in Sahlik's village are wiser than Shugdad. In a country bursting with jewels, the most sensible thing to do is play marbles with them."

"You're right," said Kayim. He sighed ruefully. "As a public versifier, I never expected to see riches in such quantity. Now, alas, I'm afraid I've lost interest in becoming wealthy. With an itch to be rich, only fools value jewels. Up to my ears in diamonds and I simply don't care."

The Bishangari staff officers were already in one of the largest chambers when the Queen's party arrived. Torches blazed around a divan and maps had been spread on the ground before it. Among Nur-Jehan's high councillors, Lukas saw several women garbed no better than common soldiers. The Queen was greeted by Zurak, a hard-bitten, iron-bearded commander, who had been Ardashir's closest companion.

Haki, who had managed to tag along, sighted a lad scarcely more than fifteen and ran, squealing joyously, to throw his arms around him. Then he beckoned to Lukas:

"Al-Ukash, here is my brother Yussuf!"

The lad had the same gray eyes as his younger brother, but fortunately was less talkative. He ceremoniously thanked Lukas for rescuing Haki. Then, his face grave, he turned again to the outspread maps.

"What's this?" muttered Lukas to Nur-Jehan. "Do you include boys in your War Council?"

"This time you are the one speaking too hastily," the girl answered. "Yussuf is one of my most brilliant officers."

Protesting bitterly, Haki was commanded back to his post with the horses. As the leaders gathered around the maps, Nur-Jehan spoke quickly and precisely, telling of Lukas and why he had come. In turn, Lukas gave an account of what had happened in Jannat.

"Much of this is known to us," said a woman whose black hair had been braided and bound around her head in the same fashion as the Queen's. "We have also learned that the King of Abadan was held prisoner there."

"What of Nahdir Aga?" Lukas asked. "We left the

house of Namash in flames. Beyond that, I know nothing."

"The Commander of Guards is dead. He has not been replaced. Shugdad Mirza has taken full personal command. He and the main body of his army are within a day's march of here."

"But you won't engage him?" said Lukas. "I've been told that your strength lies in movement. Will you withdraw your companies? If you don't, it seems to me you'll have to accept heavy losses."

Nur-Jehan and Yussuf had been poring over one of the charts. The girl raised her head and spoke in a flat voice:

"What we have to accept is far more grievous. The village people have already abandoned their homes. Most have sought refuge in the valleys around Umm al-Raas. But even there they will not find safety. Nor shall we. Shugdad has defeated us."

CHAPTER

❈❈ *21* ❈❈

*L*ukas stared at the grim faces of the Council, then turned to Nur-Jehan.

"How can you say that? Your people haven't even tried to stop Shugdad."

Nur-Jehan did not reply, but Yussuf drew Lukas closer to the map. The lad's gray eyes shone with a cold, bitter light as he unsheathed a dagger and pointed to the lines covering the chart:

"The King of Abadan has perhaps not been informed of the disposition of Shugdad's army. Here, from Jannat al-Khuld—"

"I don't know Shugdad's plan," Lukas broke in, "but there's no way I'll believe he's won a battle without turning a hand."

"What Yussuf means to tell you," said Nur-Jehan, "is that with or without a battle, the outcome will be much the same. It is true. Our greatest strength, indeed our only strength, lies in striking swiftly first in one place then another; in surprise, in quick, sharp attack. For us to stand in pitched battle, our numbers against Shugdad's, would be fatal. But this is exactly what he plans."

"Don't play his game, then," returned Lukas. "Do as you've always done."

Nur-Jehan shook her head. "The decision is not so easily made. Shugdad has come into the Ramayan in great force, from Jannat straight toward Umm al-Raas. He will soon reach the tableland at the foot of the mountain. It is there he wishes to make us fight. And if we are to do so, it is the only place we can make such a stand."

Lukas frowned. "What if you don't engage him at all?"

"Then his forces will simply overrun Bishangar. Whether or not he takes Umm al-Raas or lays siege to it, Bishangar is cut in half. Our cavalry, our small companies of foot soldiers, these will become no more than gadflies on a horse's flanks. To bite, to sting a little, but easily brushed away."

"The situation is clear to all of us," said Yussuf, "as it would be to the King of Abadan had he been instructed by his own officers or his Vizier."

"Versifying's my trade, not viziering," Kayim put in. "These chess games of yours: that's all very well, with your lines and marches and sieges. The only sensible question is what will you do next?"

"What we shall mainly do, Abadani, is die," the iron-bearded Zurak answered harshly. "Our only choice is to strike this army now, even within the hour. Fall upon them with every detachment, let cost what it will. We shall kill as many as we can. My companies, I promise, will take more than their share."

Nur-Jehan said nothing, but Yussuf nodded agreement and the Bishangari officers murmured approval.

"Wait!" cried Lukas. "You talk of losing your own lives. What of the Abadanis?"

Yussuf turned a cold smile on Lukas. "The King does not seem to grasp the nature of war: the destruction of the enemy. Be assured, the Abadanis will die in great number."

"They're my people," returned Lukas. "You speak of killing them. That's not why I came here. I'm trying to save lives, not see them lost."

"And what have you brought us to do this?" demanded one of the women commanders, looking scornfully at Lukas. "What army do you lead, O King?"

"His concern is for the Abadanis," Zurak burst out. "You heard this from his own mouth. He can have no place in this Council."

"Are you so bound on killing each other?" cried Lukas. "All this talk of giving your lives. It's noble, heroic, honorable, and I've heard it somewhere before. I'd almost think you enjoy the idea! Do you truly want a war? Can you see nothing else?"

"That, my friend," muttered Kayim, "appears to be one of the limitations of the military mind, whichever side it happens to be on."

"The King of Abadan has found something that escaped my notice." Yussuf gave a mocking bow. "Does the King choose to enlighten us?"

"Yussuf, my lad," replied Lukas, "I don't question your maps and diagrams and all you say will happen. My Court Astrologer would understand them better than I. Least of all, do I question your bravery. Only sometimes it doesn't work. You need something else that's more in my line. When it comes to that, where I was born we have a saying: Don't teach your grandmother to suck eggs."

Zurak snorted. "We speak of death. The King of Abadan speaks of eggs."

"You have taught me much," Nur-Jehan said to Lukas. "Will you now teach me how to die?"

"I'll teach you how to come out of this alive, or try to," said Lukas. "Let me take The King's Royal Camels and The Queen's Own Goats."

"The King claims a deep knowledge of eggs," said Zurak. "Is he also expert in livestock?"

"My own company and the Queen's troop," Lukas explained. "If we go quickly, we can meet Shugdad before he comes to the tableland."

"With those few," put in Yussuf, "you cannot turn aside an army."

"I know Shugdad," answered Lukas. "At least, I

hope I do. No, I don't expect to turn the army aside, though I'll do it if I can. But there's one thing that may turn Shugdad and keep him on the run till I let the army see I'm still alive. A red rag to a bull."

"First eggs, then camels, goats, and now a bull," growled Zurak. "Your words have no meaning."

"Then call it bait," said Lukas. "The only bait Shugdad will strike at: Kasha, King of Abadan."

The plain before Umm al-Raas stretched more like an expanse of shallow steps than the flat surface of a table. At first glance, Lukas had judged it to be smooth. As he rode from the foot of the mountain to the rocky pass, he realized the ground was broken here and there by long slabs of stone half-sunken in the earth. The most heavily wooded area was a crescent of scrubby beeches; there he ordered Hassan's company and the Bishangari troop into position while he trotted his mount to the far edge of the trees.

The steed, pawing restlessly and snuffling at the ground, was the tall stallion, Rakush. Nur-Jehan had insisted on his taking her beloved animal. Haki, wordless for the first time, had lost no time in saddling the horse.

"Rakush will give all you ask of him," Nur-Jehan had said. "I value him as my life. No less do I value his rider."

Lukas waited, straining his eyes toward the cliffs. The companies were well hidden. Kayim had demanded to be among them, though by now Lukas could imagine the versifier's laments growing with each passing moment. Osman and Hassan were at the head of the Abadanis. Haki, refusing to be left behind, was with his brother and Zurak, who had stationed themselves beside Nur-Jehan. Not only to guard the Queen, Lukas thought, but as much out of distrust of the Abadanis and perhaps himself.

The Queen's Council had at first disapproved his plan. Only after much argument did they reluctantly agree; even Zurak finally admitted it might work. The Council had also urged the Queen to remain in the cavern. In this, Lukas sided with the Council. In the end, however, Nur-Jehan had her way.

Sunlight dappled the ground in the beech wood. Although foliage shaded him against glare and heat, he was drenched in sweat and his legs ached. Scouts had reported Shugdad and his advance guard no more than an hour away. Lukas, uneasiness growing, feared they might have halted or at the last moment chosen a different line of march. Before he could dismount to venture a closer look on foot, he stiffened and caught his breath at the sight.

The advance party had come suddenly to the edge of the plain. At their head, with his staff officers around him, Shugdad bestrode a golden stallion. The flanks of the animal gleamed like the Vizier's breastplate. Shugdad reined in his mount and surveyed the stony expanse. Lukas froze in the saddle. Shugdad was pointing not toward Umm al-Raas but the woodland. With alarm,

Lukas realized the Vizier intended first to bring up his main body and occupy the forest. One of the staff captains and a flag bearer had already turned and were riding back through the pass.

Lukas dared wait no longer. He kicked his heels against the flanks of Rakush and clung with all his strength as the animal surged through the beeches and galloped straight for the Grand Vizier.

Shugdad's horse reared. His officers cried out and one drew sword at sight of the lone mounted figure streaking toward them. Lukas galloped on, wheeling Rakush only when close enough to be sure the Grand Vizier had recognized him.

Shugdad knew him instantly. Lukas glimpsed the bearded face twist with rage. He could hear his roar as Shugdad, throwing all caution to the mountain wind, snatched out his blade and spurred after him.

Close by the edge of the woodland, Lukas turned Rakush and reined up in full view of the Grand Vizier, who had already outdistanced his officers. At this final taunt from Lukas, the Vizier lashed his heaving mount to a faster gait. Lukas raced into the cover of the trees, Shugdad in pursuit.

By now, Nur-Jehan's and Hassan's companies should have swung in behind the Grand Vizier: some to cut off his retreat; others to block and delay any movement by his advance guard. If the Vizier could thus be captured, the Bishangaris would gain precious time without bloodshed; for Lukas intended to take one final gamble: that the army of Abadan would obey King Kasha, not the treacherous Shugdad.

But there was no sign of the Queen's party. In horror, Lukas understood his plan had gone awry. He had turned too quickly into the woods and was galloping not closer to safety, but farther away.

Before he could halt Rakush and change course, the stallion checked at a barrier of fallen trees. Lukas pitched from the saddle. His foot caught in the stirrup. Rakush turned aside and stopped immediately.

Shugdad, meanwhile, had plunged into the woods. He cried out in triumph at sight of the half-stunned Lukas trying to disengage himself and remount. The Vizier leaped from his horse. Sword flashing, he strode to the disabled Lukas.

A rider burst through the undergrowth. Lukas, scrambling to his feet, glimpsed no more than a figure who sprang down and raced toward him. Shugdad lifted the blade. At a cry from behind, the Vizier spun around and swung his weapon at the new assailant.

"Osman!" shouted Lukas, as the Vizier struck with all his might, beating down his opponent's sword. Lukas would have run to help, but Osman cried out, "Ride, King of Abadan! The army is on the plain. Go to them. Now, while you can!"

Osman's command struck him like a fist and flung him, against his will, astride Rakush. Lukas galloped for the edge of the woodland. The advance guard was already streaming through the passage between the cliffs.

As Lukas sped toward them, he heard hoofbeats at his back. He wheeled to see not the Grand Vizier but Osman, his face mottled with blood, who galloped past and shouted for him to follow.

Osman halted before the first ranks of Abadani soldiers. Some fell back, others drew their swords or leveled spears. Heedless of them, Osman called out in a voice that rang to the crags:

"King Kasha lives! The true King lives!" He seized something from his saddlebow. Among the Abadanis, murmurs rose and swelled.

"Will you follow King Kasha?" shouted Osman. He flung the thing into their midst. "Or will you follow this?"

Lukas glimpsed what Osman had held aloft by the hair. He turned his eyes away, stomach heaving. He heard voices shouting his name. Nur-Jehan was galloping toward him, Kayim beside her. It took some moments before he understood what they were telling him.

"Won?" murmured Lukas. "Yes, I suppose we have."

CHAPTER

❧❧ 22 ❧❧

By order of King Kasha, the army of Abadan withdrew to Jannat, where all would receive provisions for the return to their homes. Queen Nur-Jehan commanded her troops to fall back and remain beyond Umm al-Raas. While the war had ended even before it had begun, Lukas found his own work only starting. For the next two days, it seemed to him that he saw Nur-Jehan only through a hedge of officers and councillors. He himself was so bedeviled by his commanders, with documents, directives, and state papers, that he scarcely had time to eat or sleep.

"If you're going to be Grand Vizier," Lukas warned the versifier, "You'll have to do the work of one."

"Isn't it enough you won the war for everybody?" grumbled Kayim. "You'd suppose they'd at least give us a day off. More papers to sign and I think I'll resign; my fingers are weary, my eyes have gone bleary."

Among the people of Bishangar making their way back to their abandoned villages were Sahlik and Mariam. Haki's other kindred also turned up in such numbers that Lukas thought they must populate half of Bishangar. The boy talked himself hoarse describing what his benefactor had done.

Osman, wounded in his battle with the Vizier, had been put into the care of Mariam. A healer, she knew her art better than any physician in Abadan.

"You saved my life, Osman," Lukas told him, "and more than that."

"You, King of Abadan, gave mine back to me."

Lukas arranged for his General-in-Chief to be carried on a litter to Shirazan. The King's Royal Camels and The Queen's Own Goats were to escort Lukas and Kayim to the palace.

Before that, plans for a treaty had to be agreed upon. His arms loaded with parchments requiring the seals of both kingdoms, Lukas made his way to Nur-Jehan's council chamber, where officers of both sides were waiting to be informed of the King's choice of ambassadors.

"I've already sent for two councillors from Shirazan," Lukas told Nur-Jehan. "For Bishangari advisors in the palace, I was thinking of Zurak and Yussuf. Haki can go along and help his brother—" Lukas broke off. "What are we doing! The war's over. We should be celebrating. Laughing and dancing instead of sitting like a pair of stuffed owls!"

"There are serious matters," Nur-Jehan replied. "They must be settled."

"They will be, sooner or later," said Lukas. "What puzzles me is that there's always time for work and no' time for anything else. Enough is enough! To the devil with it!"

At that, Lukas tossed his armload of parchments in the air. "Out! Out! All of you!" he shouted at the officers, who fled scandalized under the snowstorm of state papers. The Queen of Bishangar made a show of protest, but Lukas saw the girl smiling behind her hand.

"Well, after all," said Lukas, "what's the good of being King if you can't have your own way?"

"The good of being a king," Nur-Jehan said, a little sadly, "is to have the least of your own way."

Lukas nodded ruefully. "I'm afraid you're right. If I taught you to be half a rascal, I suppose you can teach me to be half a king. I didn't do too well the first time around. The second doesn't seem any better."

Nur-Jehan frowned. "You have already done what no King of Abadan has done, and without bloodshed."

"What of Shugdad's blood? I wanted to capture him, not kill him."

"The cost of one life."

"I wonder," said Lukas, "if even one life lost isn't one too many. And how many before that? And how many after that? When we're gone, who knows what might happen? It's a risky place, this world of yours. Though now it's my world, too. I've given up thinking that Battisto will ever send me home. I still miss it. Diddling the baker's boy out of a few cream tarts, or sending the Mayor into fits—that's easier than ruling a kingdom. As I have no choice in the matter, I'll have to make the best of it. I'll try to be a real king, but I don't think I'll like it very much."

"You must take this now," said Nur-Jehan. From the folds of her robe, she took the gem-studded dagger and handed it to Lukas. "It is yours. I should have given it back to you long since."

"You didn't sell it along the way?" exclaimed Lukas. "You'd have gotten a fortune for it." He grinned at her. "It would have spared you a lot of sweeping."

"As it belonged to you," said Nur-Jehan, "I wished to keep it with me. Take it now before we part, King of Abadan."

"Why must the kingdoms be apart in the first place?" demanded Lukas. "Between the two of us, we'd make one good ruler."

"I must think carefully," said Nur-Jehan. "Perhaps I have no more choice than you do."

"At least come to Shirazan," Lukas urged. "Make a grand journey of it."

Nur-Jehan smiled. "Should I come to you, I shall come as your friend, not the Queen of Bishangar. That much I promise. Farewell. Go in peace."

His royal escort following him, in two days Lukas reached Jannat al-Khuld. With Kayim at his side, he rode straight for the house of Namash. His heart sank. The destruction had been worse than he imagined. The fire-blackened walls had fallen; rubble filled the court-yard where a figure idly picked among the stones. At sight of Lukas, the man scrambled toward him, threw himself on his knees, and cried out:

"Center of the Universe! May your shadow never be less! Forgive me! Have mercy! I did not know who you were."

Lukas blinked at him. "Katir! What are you doing——"

The horse trader pounded his forehead into the dust. "Spare my life! When I called you a cheat—ah, my accursed tongue should have knots in it! Pardon, O King!"

"I'm the one to ask pardon," said Lukas. "I swin-dled you out of a horse. It wasn't your horse to begin with, and it was all in good cause, but I swindled you nevertheless. I owe you for that."

"Center of the Universe," returned Katir, "you owe me nothing."

"Indeed I do, after that nonsense I made you believe. A horse finding a treasure! No wonder you were furious."

"I would have told you that night in Jannat," said Katir, "the horse did find a treasure. Only it was smaller than you promised. I followed your directions. In time, I came to a tree with a circle on it. Under the roots, a jar of gold pieces! But no gold bars! No sacks of diamonds, as that wretched beast claimed! On top of that, when I was digging, both jades ran off and left me in the middle of nowhere."

"It could have been worse," put in Kayim. "At least you were a rich man."

"All spent in three days," groaned Katir. "Wine, gambling, carousing. That nag cheated both of us, O King. But I cheated myself more than anyone. Even so, an honest horse is hard to find."

"Katir," said Lukas, "you don't still believe I talk to horses!"

"More than ever! You're King, you can do anything."

"My friend," said Lukas, "if you only knew."

Meanwhile, from a makeshift tent in the courtyard, Namash came running to make his way through the crowd gathering around the King's party.

Lukas called out and jumped down from his mount to grasp the man's outstretched hand, "Your house is ruined, but you have my word that you'll get a finer one."

"There can't be finer," Namash answered. "This is the best caravanserai in Jannat, in all Abadan!"

"As a public versifier," said Kayim, "I've put up in some less than luxurious accommodations. But if that wreck is a caravanserai, the innkeeping business has gone downhill since I've been away."

"Don't look at ruins, look at what isn't there yet,"

said Namash. "It *will* be the finest. After the fire, I had to clear the ground. That took some blisters. But what a blessing the house burned down. I'd never have found the treasure."

"Marvelous!" cried Lukas. "What was it? Gold? Gems? After what I saw in Bishangar, I can imagine it was quite a trove."

"Who cares about stones?" replied Namash. "This is worth more, a thousandfold." He led Lukas through the courtyard. "I was digging out the cellar and came on this."

"A hole?" muttered Kayim. "I never thought they brought much of a price."

Lukas peered over the edge of the pit. "You struck water!"

"It's part of the biggest underground stream I've ever seen," said Namash. "This isn't the only well. I dug another at the end of the courtyard, and I'm building a fountain, the best in Jannat. Once I'm done, every traveler between here and Shirazan will beg to stay at my caravanserai. Katir knows horses, so he'll tend the animals. But I know water, and I tell you there's plenty to spare. That stream must run all through the city. It's only a matter of tapping into it. With pipes and trenches, we can spread that water around and turn the country-side into a garden. Jannat will be as it was, and better. King of Abadan, you've made my fortune again!"

"Your best fortune's your good heart," said Lukas, "and that's something you've always had."

From Jannat al-Khuld, they rode to Bayaz, where the town turned out to cheer them and Locman welcomed them joyously.

"I know most of what happened," said the Astrologer. "Not by my calculations, but in a fashion more reliable: by messenger. Alas, my dear King, there is no way in the world I could have foreseen anything of what you accomplished."

Locman set out a feast and served it with his own hands. The Astrologer seemed more spry and in lighter spirits than when they last had met. However, when Lukas urged him to return to the palace with them, the old man shook his head:

"Forgive me, O King, but I shall be much happier staying where I am. I have given up making predictions of any kind. I should be no help to you."

"It isn't predictions I need," said Lukas, "but all the wisdom I can get."

"Your own will serve you as well as mine. As for knowing how the world will go, even an infant can foresee as much as I can. There is no plan that cannot somehow go astray, nor any pattern that cannot change before our very eyes."

"You may be right," said Lukas. "Who could have known where a drink of water would lead. Or missing the caravan for Turan. Osman trying to kill me and ending up saving my life. Perhaps there's no pattern. And yet, all the pieces fit."

Next morning, after saying his last farewell to the

Astrologer, Lukas told Kayim, "Now I think I'm ready to go home."

The versifier frowned. "That peculiar town you told me about? There's no way in the world you can find it."

"I know that," said Lukas. "I meant Shirazan. Yes, Grand Vizier, let's go home."

CHAPTER 23

Lukas sat cross-legged on the rocks. Below, the sea blazed as brightly as the sky. Kayim, nearby, was tossing pebbles into the surf. Until this day, Lukas had scarcely put his nose outside Shirazan Palace.

On the morning of his arrival, he had thrown his courtiers into an uproar by refusing the golden carrying chair and, as no King before him had done, striding on foot into the palace. Since then, he had thrown them into still greater uproar. He called Council meetings and required all ministers to attend. With Kayim's help, he wrote his own proclamations and decrees, not only to set right all Shugdad had done but also to better the laws he himself had made when he first was King.

Zurak and Yussuf had come as ambassadors. Haki, charged with aiding his brother, managed to be everyplace in the palace but where he was needed. From Nur-Jehan, there had been no word.

That afternoon, Lukas had grown suddenly weary. "Come on, Grand Vizier, I don't think the world will fall to bits if no one can find us for a little while."

"A moment's rest is all for the best," Kayim agreed. "The King and Vizier will disappear. Yes, by all means."

"That will be pleasant," put in Haki, who had been eavesdropping in the Royal Chambers. "I will send for a basket of food immediately. And you will need someone to carry it for you. I am ready, al-Ukash."

"You have errands to do for your brother," said Lukas. "Better get at them and leave the idling to your elders. Stay out of mischief and we'll all go on another outing tomorrow."

They called for their horses and rode to the cliffs. Laughing like schoolboys who just learned the schoolhouse had burned down, they scrambled to the crest. After a time, however, Lukas's high spirits sank a little. He clambered onto a boulder and sat looking down at the waves.

"Something troubles me," he finally said to Kayim. "I promised myself I'd do the best I could. Now I think I've gone at it all wrong."

"Too much work has muddled your head," said the versifier. "There's never been such a King of Abadan. Think of all you've done."

"That's what I mean. Before, the King never did much of anything, except make war and stir up trouble. Now, everybody depends on him for everything."

"Who better?" said Kayim. "Your people have never been happier."

"Yes, but what I've done, they should be doing for themselves. I'll be the best King of Abadan when they don't need any king at all."

"Oho, now I see it." The versifier winked. "Once the subjects look after themselves, the King of Abadan can find a little amusement on his own."

Lukas grinned at him. "I wouldn't complain about that. It will take a while to get them used to the idea, but they'll come to like it. And so will I. But it's strange. When I first came here, I never imagined I'd get tired of living like a king."

He pointed down to the white sand of the beach. "Do you know, that's where I was washed ashore? Right there. And on these cliffs, the place where Nahdir and his guards captured me."

Lukas climbed to his feet and picked his way along the ridge. "It was right here. I wonder how it all would have gone if Locman hadn't stopped them from killing me. Or, for that matter, if I'd been drowned before I could swim ashore. What might have happened, or might not have happened?"

He stopped and narrowed his eyes. There was a flash of white far down the beach. In a few moments, he saw clearly: the sand spurting around the hooves, the taut figure in the saddle.

"Nur-Jehan!"

Lukas shouted and waved his arms. The girl had

caught sight of him and was urging Rakush to a gallop. As she drew closer, ever more swiftly, Lukas could see her face. She was smiling, calling out to him.

He ran forward, scrambling over the boulders. He sprang onto a rock, the same one he had loosened from its socket long before. It shifted and tilted under his feet. He flung up his arms and tried to leap back. Kayim was racing toward him, hands outstretched. Nur-Jehan jumped from her steed and ran to the foot of the cliff.

Lukas hurtled downward into the sea.

※※※

Lukas threw back his head to clear the water from his nose and mouth. Battisto, half-smiling, was looking closely at him. Lukas gasped and stared wildly. He was standing on the cart, in the middle of the market square of Zara-Petra.

Everything was as it had been. The hands of the town clock had scarcely moved. The baker's boy had swallowed the last morsel of pie crust and was wiping the crumbs from his chin.

"Battisto! What have you done to me!"

The little man gave him a curious glance. "My dear lad, all I did was touch your face for a moment into a kettle of water."

"No! There was Abadan—the sea, the cliffs. Kayim. Nur-Jehan."

The mountebank shook his head. "I have no idea what you are talking about."

"Send me back! You must!"

Lukas tried to seize the iron vessel, but Battisto overturned it and spilled its contents onto the cobbles. "You see? Water from your own horse trough, nothing more."

The townsfolk, meanwhile, had begun whistling and clapping their hands impatiently, shouting for Lukas to get off the cart and let the conjurer get on with his tricks.

Battisto raised his hands. "Friends, friends, have patience. I have done my most remarkable feat, as this fine young man will doubtless agree. Who else chooses to take part? Come, step up."

"What," shouted the baker's boy, "can't you do better than stick our noses in a pot of water?"

The onlookers raised their voices in agreement. From some came catcalls and groans of disappointment. A moment later, an egg sailed through the air to shatter on the cart, narrowly missing Battisto's head.

The crowd guffawed and cheered all the louder as some of the town roughnecks snatched vegetables from the stands and hurled them at the mountebank. The ape sprang to the donkey's back. The wagon started with a jolt. Battisto, flinging his iron pot into the tent, gave Lukas a shove that sent him sprawling to the cobbles.

"Wait!" shouted Lukas, as the cart rattled off. The

onlookers had closed around him and he struggled vainly to fight his way through the crowd.

One took his arm. "Tell us, you scamp, what was that nonsense all about?"

"Let me go," blurted Lukas, trying to free himself. "He has to send me back to the palace."

"Palace?" put in the baker's boy, thrusting his face at Lukas. "What palace? Do you take yourself for a king now? That's the best yet! King Kasha!"

"King Kasha?" repeated one of the bystanders, breaking into laughter. The rest caught up the cry, dipping mock bows and curtsies, and jostling Lukas from one side to the other.

The cart had vanished when Lukas finally broke away. Shouts of "King Kasha! King Kasha!" rang in his ears as he raced from the square, paying no heed to the direction. Halting at last, he saw his steps had taken him to the carpenter's shop. He hesitated, head still whirling. Then he opened the door.

Old Nicholas was planing a board. He glanced up. "Back so soon? Don't tell me you couldn't find one sort of mischief or another."

Seeing the face of Lukas, the carpenter dropped his plane and hobbled to him. "Here, lad, what's come over you?"

Nicholas led him to the table and made him sit. "Now, then, tell me what you've been up to. Though I'm sure it's up to no good. Where did you go, eh?"

Lukas shook his head. "Far from here, Nicholas."

The carpenter laughed, though not unkindly. "To the end of town and back? Come on, my boy, something's done you a turn. You're too quiet to suit me."

"I was away," Lucas said. "Long away."

"So that's your game, to swindle food out of me. All right, I'm sorry I skimped your breakfast. I can see you need something."

When Lucas refused, the carpenter grew seriously alarmed. He sat down beside him, watching him with concern.

"Truly," Lukas said, "I was in a different place. I don't even know where it was, if it was anywhere." He tried his best to tell the carpenter what Battisto had done.

"Now I understand." The carpenter nodded. "You fell asleep in a doorway and dreamed it all."

"No," said Lukas. "It wasn't a dream. It couldn't have been. It was true. Nur-Jehan, Kayim, Haki—they were real."

"There's no folk with such names in these parts," said Nicholas. "Go on. You might as well have it all out."

Dusk was gathering by the time Lukas finished his tale. For a long while, he and Nicholas sat silently in the darkening shop. At last, the carpenter climbed to his feet and lit a lamp.

"Take your rest. I'll finish my work. Go on, to bed with you. Not in those shavings. The spare room. It's yours now, if you want it. This morning I asked you to be my apprentice. I ask you again."

"This morning," answered Lukas, "I'd have said no to you. I was happy enough. Nothing much mattered. Now everything matters much. Battisto promised a marvel. He didn't cheat me."

"There, I have to agree with you. I've known you a long time, my lad. I can tell. Whatever that peddler did or didn't do, you're not the same fellow you were. That's all for the better, I'd say. So, then, you'll be settling in and start work tomorrow."

"Nicholas, I still say no. I'm sorry. I'll miss you. But I can't stay here."

"What foolishness! I thought that ducking put some sense in your head."

"It did," answered Lukas. "I know as long as I'm here, no matter what I do, they'll still call me the town scamp. I don't know if it's better or worse, but Battisto said he'd change my life. And he did."

"Don't tell me you're going off chasing that peddler and his fancy ape."

Lukas shook his head. "Somehow I doubt I'll ever see them again. It doesn't matter. I got used to being in Abadan. I'll get used to being back again."

"You'll have to make a living," said Nicholas. "You were a king, wherever it was. There's not much call for that trade here."

Lukas laughed. "I'm satisfied if I can manage to be king of myself. Kayim was a public versifier and he got along one way or another. I can't spout doggerel as he did, but I think I could tell a tale or two."

"Go storytelling," grumbled the carpenter, "and leave all your friends?"

"Not leave them. Find them," said Lukas. "People are people. Nur-Jehan, or someone like her, must be here. And Kayim. Shugdad and Nahdir, too, I'm afraid. Where they may be, I won't know till I get there."

The town still slept when Lukas said farewell to the carpenter. He set off, crossing the bridge, bending his steps in the direction of the high road. There, he struck out again.

By daylight, he had come to the outskirts of a village. He kept on, stopping by an inn, where the innkeeper had finished taking down the shutters.

As the day promised to be fine, some travelers were sitting at a table in the courtyard. Seeing Lukas watching, they hailed him and beckoned him to join them.

"Sit down with us," said one. "You look like you've come a distance."

"So I have," answered Lukas. "Farther than I've ever been."

"In that case, you must have tales aplenty. Let's hear some to cheer us up and set us well on our way. We'd make it worth your while; food and drink, maybe a coin or two."

"A tale?" said Lukas, brightening. "I might have a few, if they suit you."

And he began:

"Once, in the Kingdom of Abadan . . ."

MS READ-a-thon— a simple way to start youngsters reading

Boys and girls between 6 and 14 can join the MS READ-a-thon and help find a cure for Multiple Sclerosis by reading books. And they get two rewards — the enjoyment of reading, and the great feeling that comes from helping others.

Parents and educators: For complete information call your local MS chapter. Or mail the coupon below.

Kids can help, too!